LOVE SCAMMED

RILZY ADAMS

RILZY WRITES

for Eric Jerome Dickey - because 'Milk in My Coffee' made a romance lover out of me.

CONTENT WARNING

Love Scammed contains brief mention of emotional and physical abuse.

CHAPTER ONE

You cannot practice law with a murder conviction.

You cannot practice law with a murder conviction.

You cannot practice law with a murder conviction.

Monae tightened her grip on her pull-on suitcase and tried to focus on her breathing but that wasn't doing a damn thing. She found the nearest empty seat in the bustling departure lounge of Miami International Airport and took a few more deep breaths but her annoyance didn't lessen.

"You cannot murder your best friend," she breathed. "You cannot murder your best friend."

The elderly man sitting next to her flashed her a look before he grabbed his coffee cup and newspaper and decided he better take his ass somewhere else.

"You cannot murder your best friend," Monae said again, more firmly this time, but then laughed mirthlessly. She *couldn't* murder her best friend. She loved that conniving bitch like a sister. Tempest was also currently in DC probably snuggled up with Chef Bae instead of at the Starbucks in Miami International Airport where they were supposed to meet up so they could fly to

Turks and Caicos for an overdue girls' trip. It would be hard to kill her from a thousand and fifty miles away.

"Help me, Lord Jesus," she pleaded much in the same way her mother used to when Monae got into trouble growing up and Beverly Alexander *knew* she was about to reign terror down on her daughter. There wasn't much terror Monae could reign down on Tempest over a video call, so she didn't bother answering her friend's twentieth call. Monae's flight from New York to Miami had already been hell since she overslept because she worked late into the night trying to finish some pesky legal submissions she didn't want hanging over her head during the five day trip. Then she got sandwiched between a feuding couple who didn't want to switch seats so they could sit next to each other but wouldn't stop swiping at each other for the entire three-hour flight. Monae was irritable as hell by the time she landed and wanted nothing more than to meet Tempest, whose flight should have landed half an hour before, and drag her to a bar so she could have a drink to soothe her nerves while they waited for their flight. But Tempest hadn't been there when she rolled up to their designated meeting spot. She tried video calling her a few times before she finally answered. The first strands of confusion started forming when Monae realized Tempest was still in bed. Monae tried to explain away the strangeness of the situation by assuming her friend had missed her flight but that didn't account for why she wasn't looking stressed at the airport trying to find the next available one. Monae did not anticipate the words that fell from Tempest's mouth. Her answer to the category *Things You Didn't See Coming* would have never been "*What is my best friend is a traitorous bitch, Alex?*". Tempest sat up in bed and moved her phone so Monae could see Russ sitting beside her before she said, "Promise you won't get mad..."

Those five words were rarely the start of anything good but the Monae from fifteen minutes ago still couldn't conceive anything worse than Tempest joining her on the trip that *she* suggested and *she* planned a bit later than expected. Monae from fifteen minutes ago was a naïve and clueless bitch.

"What's happening, Temp?" she'd asked.

The small, timid glance Tempest shot Russ before her boyfriend pulled her closer as if trying to support her should've been the second clue that the math wasn't mathing.

"I just want you to know we did this with the purest of intentions."

And that was the third clue.

"Temp?"

This time panic actually started creeping into Monae's voice. It was the kind of panic people felt after the cashier ran their card for a second time and the fact it was insufficient funds and not a mechanical error causing the card to be declined started to click. Yet, Monae had hoped the third swipe would do the trick and set everything right in her world again. That perhaps the math wasn't mathing because she forgot to carry the one. But then Tempest opened her mouth and shattered all of that. Monae's hands had instantly started shaking so much she dropped her phone straight to the floor. Tempest's ass was lucky all those Casetify ads at the start of the Bailey Sarian videos she was prone to watch when she tried to distract herself from work were accurate about the strength of their cases. If she'd cracked her phone screen, Tempest would have to add another thing to the list of things she could never live down.

"You cannot murder your best friend," Monae said again, continuing to take those deep breaths through her nose that were supposed to help calm her down. They weren't working. Period. Her phone vibrated but this time it was from someone Monae actually felt like she could speak to even though she knew Wynn was calling at the behest of her ex-best friend.

"Were you in on this mess?" Monae asked before Wynn could even get a word in. Her friend removed her glasses and wiped them on her lab coat. She looked tired and stressed as hell, typical

Wynn. Monae decided that, much like during University, Wynn didn't have the energy or inclination to participate in any shenanigans.

"Not me finally stumbling back to my office after a complicated delivery to find Temp blowing up my phone talking about shit that truly made no sense to me. Y'all were really planning a girls' trip behind my back? Am I the third best friend in this equation or no?"

Monae groaned. "Wynn, is now really the time?"

Wynn placed her chin into her palm. "It sure as hell is. If you'd included me there's no way Tempest would've gotten away with this crazy shit. And let's be clear. This is some crazy, crazy shit. Even by Temp's standards."

"It was last minute and she said she ran it by you and you were too busy," Monae said. "Which, come on Wynn, is pretty on brand for you. You disappear for weeks at a time. I didn't have a reason to suspect it."

Wynn rolled her eyes. "Touché. Just answer her calls, Whip. I don't need her calling my phone bawling again."

Concern pricked through the anger Monae felt. "Wait. She's feeling guilty enough to cry? Temp never cries."

Wynn chuckled. "That's getting a whole lot easier these days."

"These days?"

Her friend propped her phone up somewhere on her desk and started fixing herself a cup of coffee. "We need to reinstitute the group chat because our three-way communication skills suck." She paused for a while before she said, "Although technically I don't know this because I'm a friend. I'll leave Temp to tell you when she's ready."

"What are you talking about?"

"Aht Aht," Wynn laughed. "Back to the topic at hand. Temp said she paid for everything, right? Just change your ticket and go home."

"Do you know how many hours of overtime I put in so I could enjoy this trip?"

Wynn shrugged. "Then go."

"Did Tempest tell you what she did? That she had no intention to come on this trip at all? That this was some elaborate scheme to set me up with some guy I've never even laid eyes on?"

Wynn nodded. "Yes, but come on, he's Russ' favorite cousin. And pretty hot and sweet if I say so myself. If you're worried about your safety you don't have to."

"I didn't think she'd orchestrate a five-day blind date in friggin' foreign country if she was worried about my safety," Monae said.

"Okay great," Wynn replied. "So... if you're looking forward to the vacation anyway, just go. What's the worst thing that could happen?"

"She only booked one room," Monae said.

Wynn's reaction was not what she expected. Her friend leaned back in her chair and laughed long and hard for a full minute before she said, "I hear it's got two beds."

CHAPTER TWO

"You play too much," Hudson chuckled as he eased into a booth at the sushi restaurant in Miami International Airport's departure area where he was meant to meet his cousin for a last minute trip. When Russ told him he was interested in trying to expand *Fusion* to Providenciales, an island in the Turks and Caicos, he'd laughed and asked his favorite cousin if he couldn't bring the restaurant to New York first. He was proud as hell of Russ, though. His cousin had a vision and did everything necessary to ensure its execution was flawless. According to Russ, the five-day trip would include scouting for possible locations, meeting a legal team and visiting the competitors, which roughly translated to eating a lot of good food in a scenic place. And why would he say no to that? Hudson was surprised Russ would choose to schedule the trip to include Valentine's Day weekend because his cousin's nose was wide open for his woman but he was quick to brush off Hudson's curious questions. Instead, Russ reminded Hudson of how hard he'd been working over the last two months organizing the opening of his photo gallery in Manhattan. It was the culmination of a dream Hudson had been chasing since he was a teen. Russ was right. He had been working hard as fuck and needed a break, so Russ' impromptu trip invite seemed like a timely blessing.

"I'm actually serious," Russ' deep voice came through the phone again, just as the server headed to the table.

"Can I have an extra menu please?" Hudson asked. "I'm waiting for someone."

"That person isn't me, though," Russ said after hearing the exchange. "Monae's coming on the trip with you. She should be on her way to the restaurant to meet you now. Let's just say she's not pleased with the turn of events. She thought she was going on an anti-Valentine's Day girls' trip with Temp up until her plane landed in Miami."

The seconds ticked by as Hudson took the time to process what his cousin was saying. Hudson thought Russ had to be messing around when he first told him there had never been a business trip planned but that he was just trying to lure him to Turks and Caicos so he could finally meet Monae. Tempest had been trying to set him up on a blind date with her elusive friend since shortly after Hudson moved to New York for work. Monae wasn't having it and after a while Hudson had forgotten all about it. Apparently Tempest and Russ had not.

"Please tell me you're just fucking around," Hudson said again. Hudson's humor quickly faded when Russ didn't immediately start laughing.

"You cannot be fucking serious, man," he said. "You guys tricked me and an unknown woman into going on a *five-day* trip including Valentine's Day with each another after this woman rejected every offer of a blind date between us? You out of your black ass mind or something?"

"It seemed like a good idea at the time," Russ said.

"I'm definitely telling Granny on you as soon as I hang up here."

Russ' mouth dropped open. "Aye, there's absolutely no need for such extreme measures but don't hang up yet. Monae's refusing to pick up Temp's calls and my love is absolutely hysterical right now. You know I can't have that. Stay on until Monae gets there so Temp can talk to her."

"So you've fucked me over and now you're giving me orders?" Hudson asked with incredulity filling his voice.

"Don't be like that, bruh. We honestly thought it was going to be a cute made for Hallmark type shit."

Hudson massaged the back of his neck. "Yeah, it's official. You've been loved up for too long. Nothing about this was a good idea. A recipe for disaster, maybe. Some damn chef you are."

Russ started saying something but Hudson cut him off when he noticed a woman stalking into the restaurant. He hadn't seen photos of Monae before but he didn't need to have seen her before to know this was her. The woman was angry. Nah. Angry seemed like too tame of a word to describe the raging tornado stalking into the restaurant, dragging her carry on behind her with an aura fierce enough to scare the Devil. What the hell did Russ get him into? She looked around the restaurant for a split second before her hazel eyes locked on him. She filled the fuck out of the navy blue sweatpants and crewneck sweatshirt she wore but Hudson didn't have much time to appreciate that before she narrowed her eyes. He didn't think she could hold that suitcase with a tighter grip than she already had but somehow Monae managed as she moved towards him. He flashed a look towards his phone, hoping his stupid cousin could see just how annoyed he was. She flopped next to him in the booth and glared at him. "I hope you weren't in on this."

"As far as introductions go," Hudson said. "That needs work. You don't even know who you're talking to."

Monae made a face and gestured across the nearly empty restaurant. "You're the only Black guy sitting here on his own. I'm good with my odds, Hudson."

"I was played just like you were," he said after a few seconds of watching her sitting there – back straight, nostrils flared with enough attitude radiating off her to set his nerves on edge. He took a deep breath and gave her a bit of grace. She'd just found herself in a very uncomfortable situation and was still reeling from it.

"Look," he said. "I don't know what my cousin told you about me but I'm not so hard up for women that I'd ever be involved in stupidity like this."

"We can hear you guys."

Tempest's voice pulled him back to the phone he was holding. She'd taken Russ' phone and was sitting up in bed. It was obvious she'd been crying but Hudson wasn't quite sure if that made him any more willing to cut either of them slack. He'd entertained the possibility of just leaving but he'd already checked the bag with most of his camera equipment in for the connecting flight and Hudson didn't know what hoops he'd have to jump through to retrieve it. Frustration rolled through him again. He couldn't believe two leveled headed adults really thought anything about this was a good idea.

"Can you turn the phone to Monae, please?" Tempest asked. His cousin's girlfriend was an attorney turned entrepreneur turned business mogul and Hudson had never heard such timidity in her voice. He glanced at Monae who was shaking her head.

"Temp, I'm not sure she wants to talk to you and I think she's looking for an excuse to stab me."

"Whip, you stole my boyfriend and I forgave you so the least you can do is give me a chance to say sorry. Stop being a bitch."

Monae grabbed the phone from him and started arguing with Tempest about her knowing damn well some man named Dario played them both before some of the anger she'd been holding on to so tightly seemed to dissipate.

"I'm really mad at you, Tempest. Neither of the choices you've left me with is particularly appealing right now."

She glanced at Hudson briefly as if to apologize for calling him a non-appealing choice and he shrugged to remind her that she wasn't a particularly appealing choice either. He took a good look at Monae as she and Tempest continued their back and forth. The thing was, Monae would have been a very appealing choice if Tempest and Russ had allowed them to meet naturally without all of the cloak and dagger bullshit. Her golden brown skin looked sun kissed and Hudson wondered if she would taste like the caramel she resembled if he brought his lips to her cheek. Her lips were thick, full and sensuous even though all he'd seen her do for the past fifteen minutes was frown, pout and try not to smile when Tempest managed to pull on their familiarity with each other to lighten the mood. Hudson couldn't stop staring once he started cataloguing bits and pieces of her. The hazel eyes, which seemed to betray every emotion she ever felt, the beauty spot just above her top lip, the way her straight hair, pulled away from her face into a low ponytail, showcased just how the individual features of her face came together to form a result that could only be described as stunning. No wonder she resisted every effort Tempest made to set them up on a blind date. Monae was probably trying to dodge men left and right as it was. She rolled her eyes at something Tempest said, a shadow of a smile crossing her face. Hudson couldn't stop thinking about how fun she'd be to photograph and his hands itched to pull out the small camera he'd packed into his knapsack. Suddenly, spending five days with Monae seemed very alluring but he couldn't figure out if her showing up to the restaurant meant she intended to follow through with the trip.

"I've been spending the last forty-five minutes trying to remind myself that I love your ass too much to kill you," Monae was saying when Hudson finally tuned back into the conversation.

"You definitely can't kill me," Tempest responded. There was a small pause before she said, "I've still got another seven months of incubating your niece or nephew to go."

The instantaneous joy that spread across Monae's face was a sight to behold. Her lips finally pulled back to reveal a smile that literally stole his breath.

"I cannot believe you decided to drop a pregnancy announcement on me to save your skin," Monae said, but the light, musical sound of her laughter filled the space between them.

"But did it work though?" Tempest teased.

"For now," Monae hedged. "We still need to have a talk about how *not okay* this was."

Tempest sighed. "Hudson, come round so I can talk to you too."

He waited for Monae to indicate she had no problems with him scooting closer to her. She angled the phone so they both fit in the frame.

"Y'all look just as cute together as I thought you would. Don't they, babe?"

Russ' bigheaded self popped up on the screen and gave them a thumbs up. "Too bad they stubborn alike."

Tempest cleared her throat when she realized neither Hudson nor Monae were far enough removed from the situation to find the teasing funny.

"Look," she said. "We had the best of intentions but we obviously went about the execution in the worst way possible. Russ has gone ahead and changed the hotel reservation to two rooms. I'll email you guys the details, Whip. We're also going to go the extra mile to show how sorry we are by covering your expenses while you're there. You guys get a free trip out of this and you don't even have to see each other for the next five days if you don't want to. Whip, you can have all the spa days you can stomach and Hudson you can go take all the photos you want. I'd say it's a win-win situation but I don't feel like me and Russ are doing much winning. Is that enough groveling for you? I'm giving y'all a free vacation *and* a baby!"

This time Hudson couldn't help but laugh. "Temp, what you're not going to do is try to use my niece or nephew to score any forgiveness points."

"Yeah," Monae chipped in, beaming at the phone. "The money we're going to blow on your dime will be enough."

CHAPTER THREE

Monae laughed at the way Tempest's face fell at her idle threat that she and Hudson were going to spend all her money. Her friend was dramatic as hell. Monae couldn't begin to make a dent in Tempest's bank balance in five days unless she tried to buy one of those expansive villas she'd seen when she scrolled through Instragram photos of Providenciales.

"Am I forgiven yet?" Tempest asked. Monae chuckled. Her friend was nothing if not persistent and that was probably why she was able to launch a successful hair and skin care business when everyone thought she was insane to walk away from a legal career.

"Homicide is off the table," Monae said. "But we *will* talk about this when we get back because I can't have you thinking you can pull a stunt like this again."

Tempest made the sign of the cross. "Oh no. I've learned my lesson and will be staying my ass out of your love life going forward and I won't drag Russ into anymore schemes so I guess you're safe too, Hudson."

"Better be."

Monae glanced at Hudson, fighting down a smile when she realized they'd spoken simultaneously.

Tempest sucked her teeth. "Look at y'all taking the words out each other's mouth and fighting my judgment that I knew from the jump you'd be perfect for each other. Have a good solo vacation or whatever."

Then Tempest had the audacity to disconnect the video call without giving either of them a chance to respond.

"Wait, did that end with Tempest being annoyed *at us*?" Hudson asked. Monae struggled against being drawn to the deep baritone of his laughter. Hudson was an attractive man and physically he was *just* what she was into. He was tall with enough lean muscle that she knew he spent some time in the gym but not bulky in the way most men who were into working out were. His dark skin contrasted nicely against his straight, white teeth and light stubble covered his jaw instead of having a fully-fledged beard. He was wearing a polo shirt but Monae couldn't stop looking at the tattoo of bold geometric lines on his left arm that extended to his elbow. Monae found tattoos so damn sexy and she wondered if it extended as far as his shoulder, back or chest.

"How are we going to start spending Temp's and Russ' money?" he asked. She slowly turned her attention away from how sexy his grin was.

"I don't know about you," she said. "But I could definitely use something to drink."

Hudson signaled for the server. "You and me both."

~

She and Hudson exchanged small talk as they tried to decide on what they wanted to drink and eat. It wasn't 10 AM yet but the restaurant was already serving a full menu so she suggested they just ate there instead of trying to find somewhere else.

"What do you want to get after the miso soup? I don't really fuck with edamame much but gyozas are my favorite," he said glancing up from his menu. "And then maybe we can share a platter? It's a great assortment and good headway to spending all of Temp's and Russ' money."

Monae laughed out loud. "I like the way you think. What are you drinking?"

"Do you mind if I order for us?" he asked. "I'm not on some chivalrous shit but I've got an idea I think you'd like."

"Have at it," she said. "We've got nothing but time and apparently an unlimited budget."

"Say less."

He signaled for the server and gave her a bright, friendly smile as he ordered up two miso soups, gyozas and one of larger sushi platters. Then he ordered a bottle of champagne and a glass of orange juice, requesting that the server brought two champagne flutes.

"Mimosa time," he grinned. "I can't think of a better way to start a modified girls' trip than being mimosa drunk before noon."

"You ordered a single glass of orange juice for a bottle of champagne."

She couldn't stop giggling now. *Giggling*. Monae couldn't remember the last time she'd giggled without being wine drunk.

He shrugged. "The orange juice is just to add color, babe."

Her smile widened. *Oh. He was good.*

Monae wasn't sure if it was the half bottle of champagne she'd had or the pleasant fullness of the sushi platter and appetizers, but she was more relaxed than she'd been in months. And that was saying a lot because a few short hours ago she was probably more stressed out than she'd ever been.

"Do you think you were extra mad because of how much you were looking forward to seeing Tempest?"

She swirled the mimosa in her glass, took a sip and nodded. Monae appreciated his insightfulness because neither Tempest nor Wynn seemed to get *that*. She was never truly worried about her safety and she knew she had the option of either just going home, spending the five days in Miami or exactly what Tempest eventually offered: having a vacation separate to Hudson. None of those options made up for just how much she had been looking forward to being in the same physical space as her friend after so many months. She'd been excited as hell when Tempest brought up the girls' trip two weeks ago after Monae complained about another relationship ending after less than a month. It stung knowing that all the things Temp had said about missing spending time with her were probably just in aid of getting her to agree to come on the trip *knowing* she was setting it up so the man Monae had been dodging for nearly six months would be there too.

"You do know somewhere in their deranged minds this was an act of love, yeah?"

She chuckled. "Deranged is right."

Hudson clinked his champagne glass to hers. "Their hearts were in the right place. Now their wallets are right where they need to be."

Monae laughed so hard she almost choked on the mimosa she'd been taking a sip of. She clinked her glass against his again. "Now that deserves another toast!"

CHAPTER FOUR

The flying time was less than two hours between Miami and Providenciales but Monae somehow managed to drift right off to sleep as soon as the plane reached a cruising altitude. Hudson alternated between being worried she'd wake up and catch him staring at her like a creep and being unable to keep his eyes off of her as she slept. There was something deeply vulnerable about sleep. It was one of the only times a person just... was. The mask so many persons wore fell off and Hudson thought it was a beautiful thing. He'd planned to spend the flight reading but Hudson spent most of the time just taking her in. Taking in the way her eyelashes almost brushed against the very tops of her cheekbones, the way those full lips quivered during sleep and the small crescent shaped scar on her chin. She was so damn gorgeous and Hudson was struck, again, with annoyance that Russ and Tempest chose the heavy-handed route. He didn't know much about Ms. Sleeping Beauty, but he knew she seemed stubborn as fuck. He had the gut feeling she would keep him at arm's length just on principle no matter how well they got along. He'd finally gotten into the fantasy novel he'd brought along by the time Monae shifted. She stretched her hands above her head, yawned and winced at the kinks in her muscles from how she'd been folded into the seat.

"How long have I been out?"

The captain interrupted before Hudson could respond, announcing the start of the descent into Providenciales.

"Looks like I was right on time," she grinned, leaning over so she could look out the window. Her body brushed against his as she marveled at the vivid turquoise waters.

"This is gorgeous," she breathed. "I watched so many videos that I had an image of what this would be like but... wow."

Hudson couldn't concentrate on the beauty of the island as it came into better view. He couldn't focus on the way the turquoise water deepened into blue, the pristine white sand or the lush greenery when Monae was pressed so closely into him he could feel the softness of her breasts against his arm while the light, floral perfume she wore had his hands itching to pull her closer. Damn. It was going to be a long five days. Hudson shook his head at the thought. He didn't even know if Monae would be interested in spending any time with him once they'd navigated their way to the hotel and went to their separate rooms. But he found himself hoping she would. Hudson was intrigued by the woman sitting next to him and by what it was about the thought of them together that made his mostly levelheaded cousin act the fool.

~

Monae was too caught up with gazing out the window to feel self-conscious about the fact Hudson had likely seen her dribble while she slept the flight away even though she usually found herself self-conscious about everything. She started feeling the first flutters of excitement since all of this chaos happened. She couldn't wait to put on one of those bikinis she packed and lay out next to the pool with the most sickeningly sweet alcoholic cocktail she could order.

"I can't wait to get my camera out," Hudson was saying. "There are so many cool shots waiting to happen."

"Oh? You're into photography?"

He smirked. "You could say that."

Gentle amusement crept across his face and Monae frowned, feeling like she'd missed something. She tried to bring everything Tempest had told her about Hudson to mind but couldn't remember much other than he was creative and *just Monae's type*.

"Why do I get the feeling you're laughing at me?" she asked fixing her gaze on his.

He just chuckled. "Definitely not doing that. I'm only just realizing what a shitty job my cousin and Tempest did at selling me to you. No wonder you turned down meeting up with me..." Hudson paused to think. "... thirteen times."

"It wasn't anything against you. I told Temp I didn't want to be set up with anyone. I tank my love life just fine on my own."

"I feel like there's a story there but I won't push just yet," he said. "I've got five days to find out."

He said it in the same deep, soft-spoken, but authoritative, voice he'd been using all day but Monae didn't need any legal instinct to appreciate how loaded the casual statement was. Did he have five days to find out? She knew Tempest probably expected them to go their separate ways once they landed on the island and Monae thought it would be an easy choice to make. She wasn't one of those people who didn't know how to enjoy their own company so a solo vacation was appealing. But so was the thought of spending time with Hudson. Especially if their impromptu sushi and mimosa brunch was any indication of how much fun they could have together. It should be a simple choice but Monae couldn't fight her petty desire to opt to spend the time by herself just so Tempest didn't get the satisfaction of thinking her misguided plan might have worked but for Monae's stubbornness. Tempest would just be reenergized in her efforts to pair them off if she and Hudson popped back up from the trip comfortable with each other. Yes, she knew her friend would probably never try to do anything so sneaky or underhanded again but Tempest knew how to make a damn nuisance out of herself when she wanted to.

You won't only bite off your nose to spite your face. You'd gouge out your damn eyeballs too.

Those were the angry words her last serious ex-boyfriend – ex-fiancé, really – spat at her as she packed her shit to leave. Robert was wrong as hell about *that* situation but he was right that sometimes her stubbornness knew no bounds. Monae took a deep breath and hoped she wouldn't regret her decision.

"Yeah," she whispered, holding the gaze of his deep brown eyes. "You got five days to try to get it out of me. Try, being the operative word. It won't take more than ten seconds for you to clear up the question I asked you, though."

"Oh that? I'm a photographer," he said. "As in, it's not my hobby but my job."

"That's dope," Monae said. She could feel the smile spread across her face. Despite going into the law and loving the shit out of it, Monae was obsessed visual imagery. She'd pick up a magazine before she would pick up a book during her downtime. She loved puzzles, coloring books with complicated patterns, did amateur photography and even dabbled in painting. *Damn Tempest.*

"Do you have a website or something so I can go creep your work?"

There was that little smile again. What was she missing? The plane had begun taxiing on the runway when it hit her.

"You're a big deal, aren't you?" she said. "That's what's happening here."

His shy smile was charming as fuck when he said, "Only if you're into photography."

"Which I am," she insisted. It was his turn to look intrigued and Monae wondered how much Tempest and Russ told him about her. "Tell me which images of yours I would have seen."

"Probably the Rihanna shoot," he said casually. A little too casually. Casually like he photographed celebrities all the time. "The one I did for *Process Magazine*."

She knew exactly which one he was talking about. There were a variety of bright shots with an excellent manipulation of lighting but it was the black and white portraits that had gone viral on just about every social media platform a year ago. It'd even propelled her to search out the photographer and she purchased a few prints. One of the prints, a black and white shot of a lake that was both haunting and serene, hung in her office. The final pieces of the puzzle fell together and Monae couldn't stop the bewildered laughter from spilling from her mouth. *Bradley Hudson.*

"Who would've thought inverting your name would be just as effective as Clark Kent putting on some glasses. You and Russ have the same last name for hell's sake. I feel like such an idiot."

His big, warm hand covered hers and Monae's breath caught a little bit in her throat. "Don't be. For whatever reason Tempest decided to tell you next to nothing."

"Temp is all for the dramatics. Now that I think about it, these set up attempts started just after she'd visited me and probably saw I had a few of your photos hanging in my apartment."

He raised a thick eyebrow. "You've bought my stuff."

She nodded. "And paid a pretty penny for it too."

He opened his mouth as if to defend the prices attached to his pieces.

"Hey," she said. "I'm teasing. I'm a strong believer in paying artists what they are worth, even if I had to remind myself I had food at home for a good three months after the fact."

He laughed. "Don't do me like that. I'm honored, though. I never know how to act around people who appreciate my work enough to actually purchase it."

"I'd act like I was the shit," Monae suggested. "Cause you kind of are."

He dragged his bottom lip through his teeth and averted her

gaze. His skin tone was too dark for him to show any of the stereotypical signs of blushing the media shoved in people's faces, but this gorgeous, talented man was sure as hell blushing. Monae had to take a deep breath to settle herself before another thought flashed across her mind.

"This is going to seem like a weird question but just roll with it."

He nodded. "Aight."

"Do you wear glasses, Hudson?"

He looked bewildered but rolled with it just as he promised he would. "Yeah, I do."

Monae squeezed her eyes shut and shook her head. *Damn Tempest.*

CHAPTER FIVE

It'd been nearly two hours since Hudson and Monae parted ways to their respective hotel rooms with a plan to rest up before they headed to the Thursday night fish fry which the taxi driver recommended while he drove them to the sprawling hotel nestled along Grace Bay. The night promised dancing, lots of food and drinks along with tons of souvenirs on sale. Hudson thought it would be a perfect way to start their Turks and Caicos vacation. He was sitting on a wicker lounge chair with the softest turquoise cushions having a few sips of tequila he'd poured into a small glass he'd taken from the mini-bar. The tequila, just as everything else in the resort, was luxurious as fuck. He quickly typed the brand into Google and chuckled at the $450.00 price tag. He couldn't imagine what the hotel's markup would be but he wasn't too fussed about it. Better Russ' wallet than his. The hotel was absolutely gorgeous. Everything from the palm tree lined drive that took them from the main gate to the reception building screamed *indulgent tropical oasis*. The marble floors were a shade Hudson could only describe as wet sand. He'd taken a good five minutes to come up with that description while he and Monae lounged on one of the wicker chairs sipping on the icy rum punch one of the staff members provided almost as soon as they sat down. They had passed the time discussing their plans for later that evening while commenting on the hotel's décor. Monae was particularly enchanted with the fresh flowers placed strategically around the lobby. He'd expected the tropical type flowers like the hibiscus and bougainvillea but there were also calla lilies and roses in large, ornate white ceramic vases. He was surprised to find a vase filled with calla lilies on a table in the small seating area of the large, ocean view room Russ rebooked him into. Hudson continued sipping his tequila on ice while he gazed out at the gentle waves crashing against the shore. He couldn't wait to go for a swim but he didn't have much time to unwind before it was time to head out to the fish fry. He had a quick shower, allowing the pulsing jets of the waterfall shower heads in the expansive glass encased shower to rain down on his back before selecting shorts and a polo shirt for the outing. He was halfway through getting dressed when his cell phone chimed. He wasn't surprised to see Russ calling.

"Hey traitor," he said good-naturedly.

Hudson could hear pots and pans banging and sizzling in the background. He wondered what his cousin was cooking up and felt his stomach grumble.

"You sound very content," Russ said. His voice was accusatory. "I guess you've warmed up to the arrangement."

"I've warmed up to the resort. This place is fancy as hell."

"Stop going on like you couldn't easily afford to stay there," Russ said, managing to convey his eye roll with the tone of his voice. "You're no struggling artist."

Hudson ignored the jab in favor of trying to get some of his questions answered. "Speaking about artists, Monae didn't even know who I was. I thought the whole point of blind dates was to actually tell the people why you think they'd match. Did Tempest really just go 'Hey my big head boyfriend has a really cute, successful cousin and I think you should meet him'? You should've seen Monae's face when she realized I was into photography and then when she realized I was Bradley Hudson. It really never had to come to all of this."

"You're marginally successful but you sure as hell ain't cute," Russ said.

"Fuck you, man," Hudson said, but he was laughing so hard he had to pause zipping up the navy blue Bermuda shorts he was wearing.

"On a serious note, though," Russ continued. "It was plain as day the more I interacted with Monae that you guys would be great together especially after what she'd been through..."

"What she'd been through?" Hudson asked, cutting Russ off. His cousin paused for a while before he said, "It's not my business to tell. But anyway, you know I *hate* the idea of setting up people because I don't like the thought of things going bad and then getting the 'well if you never introduced us' talk. I was inclined to break my own rule when Tempest started talking about how good you guys would be together and I was about to come at you with photos, references and an E-Harmony personality test."

Hudson rolled his eyes as Russ chuckled at his own lame joke before he began talking again. "Tempest put a stop to that before I could blink. She thinks the best thing about dating is slowly finding out you and someone fit. She believed you guys would trust our assessment since we both knew you so well. She didn't count on Monae just flinging every single wall up."

"So she decided she wanted to be right so bad she'd force the issue?"

"Wanted to be right?" Russ said. His voice was dripping with incredulous humor. "Temp *is* right. I think you and Monae have spent enough time together now that you're both starting to realize."

The easy way Monae made him laugh, how he could spend forever watching emotions move across her beautiful face as he listened to her speak and the steady throb of sexual attraction he'd started feeling the moment he laid eyes on her flashed through Hudson's mind.

"Crickets, huh? Don't worry. We don't plan to gloat when the inevitable happens," Russ laughed. "Well, not too much anyway. You have a good trip, little cousin. Stay blessed."

CHAPTER SIX

Monae continued to ignore her ringing phone as she sank deeper into the warm bubble bath she had less than twenty minutes to enjoy if she didn't want to be late meeting Hudson in the lobby for the time they agreed on.

Her phone had been ringing intermittently throughout the half hour she'd been relaxing in the lavender scented bath. It had to be Tempest calling and if Monae knew her friend just a little bit, she knew exactly what the call would be about. She made a face. *Damn Tempest.* She took her time moisturizing her skin with the thick vanilla and honey body butter from Tempest's line *Glow* that she couldn't do without before sliding into the green maxi dress she'd pulled out of her suitcase. She even made a point of spraying insect repellant on and ensuring she had all the bits and bobs she'd need in her bag before she returned her best friend's call.

"I was about to tell Hudson to come downstairs to check on you but I already have the answer to my question by your mere avoidance of this conversation," Tempest laughed.

"Whatever, Temp. I'm not avoiding anything. I was just trying to have a relaxing bath since it's been a long ass day."

"Uh huh. Sure, Whip. Whatever you say," Tempest said. "So this is where you admit I was right and you were wrong."

"Goodbye, Tempest," Monae said. "You don't have anything to pat yourself on your back for so I'm not even going to make myself late entertaining your smugness."

"Late for what?" Tempest asked with so much innocence in her voice Monae almost thought she hadn't already found out about the outing she and Hudson had planned. *Almost*. Except, she knew her friend better than that. If Tempest was trying to call her as soon as she figured she was settled into the hotel that probably meant she made sure Russ called Hudson too.

"I'm going for something to eat and the taxi is getting here for six," she said. "I don't want to keep the driver waiting."

"I thought you and Hudson were going to some sort of fish fry."

"Why did you ask me a question then? You're not nearly as slick as you think you are."

Tempest scoffed. "Aren't I? You trying to tell me you aren't kicking yourself for not agreeing to see him the first time I brought up the idea of a blind date"

"Goodbye, Tempest."

"The man has got Monae kryptonite written all over him. The tattoos, his low-cut hair, the stubble, the glasses, the physique – he's *all* of the physical traits you look for rolled into a man whose personality and interests are completely in sync with yours."

"It might have been helpful if you'd given me some of that information beforehand," Monae complained.

"And steal the chance for you to get to know him in an organic way? Nah. You should've trusted me."

"It had nothing to do with trust, Temp and you know it."

"I know you vowed to never meet a man on a blind date after what happened with Ian but that man was a special type of asshole. Besides, you are allowed to go back on things you once felt strongly about with new information. I've hand delivered you the perfect man and even if you end up not agreeing with me, *but you will*, Hudson is the perfect person to explore Providenciales with. Not to mention you might be able to scam your way into having your photos taken by a world-renowned photographer."

Monae chuckled. "You've should've stuck on the legal path because if convoluted arguments were a person..."

"Be grateful for my deviation, eh. If I'd stuck to law there's no way I could've afforded to be covering all of your expenses at *that* hotel," Tempest laughed and Monae joined in because her friend had a hell of a point.

"Monae?" Tempest said, her voice suddenly not as teasing as it once was.

"Mhmm?"

"This isn't about Ian, you know that right? Him and his cousin were slimy as shit but Ian didn't really affect you in any way other than being a story you love to tell at parties."

"Temp," Monae warned, hoping her friend would heed the warning in her voice and not go down the road she knew she was heading.

"If you continue allowing Robert to..."

"Stop," she said with finality in her voice. "This has nothing to do with anything other than the fact you really did me dirty scamming me into this trip."

There was a beat of silence on the line before Tempest started talking again. Monae was relieved to hear the teasing note back in her voice. "You're stuck in paradise with a hot, sensitive, talented guy who has a lot of things in common with you. Poor baby. How will you ever survive?"

"Fuck you, Tempest," Monae laughed.

"Russ is doing that just fine, beloved," Tempest shot back. "You need to see what you can get into or under over the next five days. Don't be shy, Whip. Go 'head and buss it open for my cousin-in-law."

"Goodbye, Tempest," Monae said but this time she actually

disconnected the call. Her blood heated just thinking about what it might be like to buss it open for Hudson. Tempest was wicked as hell for even putting the thought in her mind. She laughed at the thought.

"You know damn well the thought was already there," she whispered to her reflection as she checked herself over in the mirror. She sighed. It was going to be a *long* five days.

CHAPTER SEVEN

W*hen the inevitable happens.*

Russ' words weren't just on Hudson's mind. They had packed up, moved in, kicked up their feet and were resting comfortably on his brain. The absolute certainty in his cousin's voice was only rivaled by how Russ sounded when he'd awoken Hudson at an ungodly hour a few years before to tell him he'd gone to what should've been a regular degular private chef gig and ended up meeting the woman he knew he would spend the rest of his life with. He loved Russ like a brother and it was no secret Russ felt the same. That Russ seemed so secure in his conviction that something special could grow between him and Monae was enough to make Hudson really want to see for himself.

Monae strode into the lobby with her relaxed hair pulled up into a high ponytail, burgundy lipstick on her lush full lips and a dark green maxi dress hugging her hips and ass in ways that had him needing to adjust himself in his shorts. She smiled widely and waved when she spotted him before making her way over to corner where he stood next to a potted majesty palm plant that almost came up to his shoulders.

"You look... wow."

The words spilled out his mouth as she came to stand next to him. She tilted her chin so she could look up at him. "Wait... was I looking a mess before or something? You sound a little too surprised."

"Uh huh," he said. "You're the type of woman Beyoncé was talking about in 'Flawless' and I know you know that."

Her smile widened. "I know nothing but go 'head Mr. Bradley, flattery will get you everywhere."

Hudson extended his arm to Monae, smiling when she linked hers through his. "Flattery, huh? I'll be sure to remember that."

~

This was when her vacation started.

It wasn't when she woke up disoriented as hell an hour after her alarm was supposed to have gone off and then began her frenzied rush to get to JFK before her flight closed.

It wasn't when she and Hudson demolished a sushi platter and toasted to doing their best to spend as much of Russ and Tempest's money as possible.

It wasn't when she walked into her massive hotel room with the four-poster bed, claw foot standalone tub and expansive ocean view balcony.

The vacation began with her here, standing under the light of the moon, with a coconut daiquiri in her hand as she rocked side to side to the smooth reggae beats of the live band on the stage. Hudson stood so close to her that she could feel the heat from his body against her arm. She was just enjoying the beautiful melody and breezy beats of the song but she had never heard it before. Her apparent soul mate, if Tempest had anything to say about it, wasn't just vibing because the song sounded nice. Hudson knew every word and was singing at the top of his lungs as he rocked to the beat while holding a bottle of beer loosely in his hand. She'd been fully prepared to tease him but Hudson actually had a nice singing voice.

"That seems like your jam."

The band had started up with another song when he leaned down so she stood a chance of hearing him over the noise.

"My family's Jamaican and my grandmother loves Beres Hammond. 'Rock Away' is actually one of her favorite songs. Me and Russ used to have a bet about how many times she'd start randomly humming it during any given day."

They enjoyed a few more songs before they made their way through the crowd to try to sort out dinner. The crowd was surprisingly large but Monae quickly realized this was a hang out for tourists and locals alike. It was called a fish fry but there were many seafood and non-seafood choices at the different stalls lining the space.

"What you feel like getting?" she asked Hudson once they'd decided on a stall, *Mama Lou's Homecooked Food.*

"I'm down for anything as long as it isn't shrimp."

Monae's eyes widened. She brought her hand to her mouth like she was scandalized. "What did you say?"

"I don't eat shrimp. Didn't you see I left all the rolls with shrimp for you?"

"Well damn," she said. "I just thought you realized they were my favorite."

His grin was devilish. "I did notice you moan and dance a little each time you popped one into your mouth."

"I'm not even ashamed. It was *that* good."

"Ashamed for what? I thought it was cute."

Hudson's gaze met hers and he held it until she looked away, afraid he'd see a spark of whatever was fluttering around her body making her heart beat so hard she could feel the thudding in her ears.

"Shrimp reign supreme. I'm not sure what to make of your subpar taste buds," she stammered, trying to regain control of the situation. Hudson smiled lazily at her before pulling her into a good-natured side hug.

"Sea cockroaches?" he teased. "Me and my taste buds are good over here."

She rolled her eyes. "Stop with the fake news. Shrimp is the best thing you could have in your mouth."

His smile widened as his tongue swiped across his bottom lip. He didn't stop looking at her when he said, "I doubt that."

CHAPTER EIGHT

Hudson blinked against the sunlight filtering into his room. He'd barely had anything to drink but he felt exhausted as hell. He supposed that had something to do with him being barely able to sleep all night for how thoughts of Monae infiltrated his mind. He couldn't remember the last time he'd had so much fun with a woman... well, with *anyone* really. They spent the night laughing, dancing, drinking and eating good food. Hudson had started finding any excuse to touch her: a casual arm thrown over her shoulder, wrapping her small hand in his large palms so he didn't lose her in the crowd, squeezing her thigh to get her attention or leaning into her while he laughed. But it wasn't until he walked her to her room when they got back to the hotel that he finally got the chance to hug her properly. She felt so soft, so lush and so perfect pressed up against his body. He dug his fingers into her hips as he buried his chin in the crook of her neck, enjoying the sweet smell of whatever perfume she wore. If it had been the end of a date, Hudson would have backed Monae against the hotel room's door and devoured her mouth the way those pouty lips begged to be. He would have allowed his fingers to slide further down to squeeze the ass that had been mesmerizing him all night. Then, he'd take her into her room so he could prove that those sea cockroaches were definitely not the best thing he could put into his mouth. Reason outweighed the lust that had become lava in his blood, though. He reluctantly stepped out of the hug and told her to have a good night's sleep. Hudson stood there while she fumbled with her key card twice before she was able to enter her room and then returned to his own to take one of the coldest showers of his life. It hadn't done shit and he spent the rest of the night tossing, turning and resisting the urge to stroke his dick until he found relief.

He stretched and yawned through the lingering exhaustion he felt before he finally got out of bed and prepared himself for the day. It was nearly nine in the morning and although he wanted to check on Monae to see if she wanted to grab breakfast, he decided against it. He didn't want to be all up in her face. He got his favorite camera and a put a few different lenses in his knapsack. It was as good of a time as any to see what sort of shots he could capture around the hotel. It was likely he'd get a few he could edit to sell as stock images. If he was lucky, he might capture something with enough emotion and texture for him to add to one of his collections. These kinds of shoots were Hudson's favorite. He had no concepts, expectations or restraints. He would allow his curiosity to be a guiding light and see where he ended up. He threw in the film camera he brought along with him just in case he wanted to mix it up between film and digital shots.

He opted for the more casual of the four breakfast spots on the sprawling resort, grabbing a croissant with some cold cuts and a glass of orange juice. Hudson people watched for a little bit while he had his breakfast. As expected, with Valentine's Day being the next day, the resort was filled with couples of all ages and seemingly all stages in their relationship. There was one couple sitting close to the coffee bar that looked like this was *the* trip that would decide whether or not their relationship or marriage would continue. Things weren't looking good on that front. He was still watching the stiff interaction between the pair when he felt someone sit next to him.

"That's a sad looking breakfast," Monae commented as she put a plate filled with a cheese omelet, a few strips of bacon and smoked salmon on the table. Her hair was pulled back into a messy ponytail and she looked fresh faced and relaxed. He began explaining the state of his breakfast but she motioned for him to wait as she started walking to the fruit station. He groaned. She was dressed in a pair of tropical printed shorts with a white tank top. He couldn't take his eyes off her ass as she crossed the room and suddenly Lil Wayne's line about hating to see a woman go but loving to watch her leave in 'Bedrock' resonated with him. He wasn't the only one having a hard time keeping his eyes off Monae. The man over by the coffee station was steadily sinking the final nail in his relationship's coffin as his eyes tracked all of Monae's movements much to the growing irritation of his woman, who was starting to get tired of pretending she didn't notice him ogling another woman's ass.

Monae returned with a selection of fruits completely unaware of the friction she and her ass just caused in those people's relationship.

"So yeah," she continued, oblivious to the argument in progress behind her. "You were about to tell me why your breakfast looks so sad."

"It was just a warm up," Hudson said. He pointed to the knapsack on the floor beside him. "I'm going to take some shots around the resort just now and the last thing I needed to do was be suffering from the itis."

Her laughter was a beautiful melodic sound and Hudson found himself leaning into her. "The itis is just what I'm looking forward to. I plan to eat enough breakfast so I pass out for at least three hours when I get back to my room. I didn't sleep well last night."

Hudson raised an eyebrow. Did she suffer the same fate he did the night before? "How come?"

She took a bite of her omelet and did that moan and dance combo Hudson found cute at the sushi restaurant. Now it just made him painfully hard.

"Yeah, I hate sleeping in new places. It usually takes me a day or two to adjust."

He nodded. "Yeah, I used to be like that but it got a lot better once I started traveling a bit more for work."

"So I guess you slept like a baby?

"In the most literal sense," he confessed and then quickly shifted the conversation before she could delve any deeper into what he said. He entertained her with his observations about the couples around them while she finished her breakfast before walking her back to her room.

"I'll see you around," he said. "I hope you're able to get some rest."

"Thanks, Hudson. What do you want to get into today after you're done shooting?"

You, he thought but because his mother raised a gentleman he told her he wanted to go to the local brewery because the place had amazing reviews on several travel sites.

"Mind if I tag along?" she asked.

"Of course not."

He lingered in the hug he'd pulled her into after they planned to meet for lunch before they headed to the brewery. Her scent lingered on him as he scouted for the first shooting location. There were many nice spots to choose from but Hudson couldn't get his mind to focus on the task at hand. The resort was beautiful but the beauty that occupied his mind was probably curled up in bed succumbing to the effects of the itis. He pulled his phone from his pocket and shot off a quick message to Russ.

Hudson: Okay. I give it to you. Monae is... wow. I think I'm in trouble, bruh.

CHAPTER NINE

The heavy sleepy feeling that hugged Monae like a weighted blanket disappeared as soon as Hudson pulled her into his arms. God, he felt great against her body. His fingers dug slightly into her hips as he buried his chin in the crook of her neck. His warm breath rushed across her skin making her shiver. It took a lot for her to step back and watch him walk to the elevator instead of inviting him inside. *Damn Tempest.* Monae was starting to forget why she was so intent on resisting Hudson in the first place. The man was fine, talented and made her body react in ways it hadn't in a long ass time. She pushed the wanton thoughts from her mind as she undressed and sunk into the bed. The plush, white sheets must have been made of the softest cotton but sleep still didn't come. Monae was too busy thinking about Hudson. She wondered how his lips would have felt against her neck if he'd just leaned in and pressed little kisses there. She wasn't sure when she finally managed to drift off, but she awoke with a start after what seemed like only a few seconds of sleep. She glanced at her watch and swore under her breath. She'd spent so much time twisting, turning and thinking about Hudson that she fell asleep later than she'd planned to and overslept. She had less than twenty minutes to throw together an outfit before she needed to meet Hudson and she'd observed he was always prompt. He was already waiting in the lobby in shorts and a fitted white shirt holding a to-go cup with the hotel's branding of something warm in his hands. He smiled when he saw her and her stomach tightened. She couldn't hold his gaze as she remembered the nasty thoughts she'd had about him just as she drifted off to sleep. Monae stepped into his waiting embrace and stilled for a few seconds just enjoying how it felt to be pressed against him while his hands splayed against the small of her back.

"The taxi's already here," he said when she finally stepped away from him, body still buzzing from the lust that made her face hot.

The drive to the Turks Head Brewery wasn't a long one, but Monae already realized nothing was really too far away in Providenciales. They settled on the taxi returning for them in about three hours before they headed to the brewery tour. There were six people on the tour and four of them were coupled up. Monae tried her best to keep her attention fixated on the animated tour guide, Samantha, as she told them about the process of brewing beer while the seven of them stood on a platform overlooking the machinery below. She kept sneaking glances at the two couples, trying not to feel jealous at how utterly loved up they looked. She glanced back when she felt a warm hand on her shoulder to find Hudson looking down at her with warm concern in his eyes. He leaned down so that he didn't interrupt the tour guide when he asked, "You good? Your energy dropped a little bit."

She hit him with the most genuine smile she could muster and lied through her teeth by telling him she was fine. She didn't want to explain that she was finally doing exactly what Tempest said she would do. Monae was wondering what would have happened if she'd agreed to any of the million opportunities her best friend provided for her to meet Hudson. Hell, even Wynn had managed to find three minutes of free time to encourage her to go to one dinner date Tempest had been trying to set up. She'd been so damned stubborn. Now she was here half listening to the tour guide talk about the correct temperature to store beer while watching two couples being lovey-dovey around her as she tried to resist the urge to press her back against the hard planes of Hudson's chest and hope he would embrace her. All on the day before Valentine's Day. This was going to be a weird Valentine's Day even though shitty ass Valentine's Days were pretty on brand for Monae's life. She pushed her feelings down and devoted her attention to the small, interesting facts their tour guide was dishing out before they all went back to the bar for the part of the tour Hudson had been looking forward to – the beer and cider tasting. He ordered them a flight of beer before she was even properly seated on the bar stool along with some popcorn to munch on. Her mood improved instantly once the bartender with the nametag 'Doug' pinned to his chest started making and encouraging conversation between everyone around the bar. The six of them shared their experiences from the fish fry the night before and the bartender suggested two or three restaurants for them to check out. Marianne and Luther, the newlyweds, also lived in New York and so there was some back and forth about how great it was to escape the awful weather. Everything was going great until the bartender poured his own flight of beer and then turned to everyone with a cheeky smile.

"I love when we get couples so I can do my favorite challenge. I want each couple to tell us how you met," he gestured to their tour guide. "Sam and I will choose the most interesting story and the winning couple gets the next two rounds free."

Monae hadn't even realized she'd stiffened until she felt Hudson caressing the small of her back. He leaned into her and whispered, "We got this one."

She made a face. "We're not a couple."

Hudson shrugged. "Very small detail."

Monae started telling him being a couple was the entire point of the challenge but stopped when the retired couple, Donny and Bertha, started talking about how they met when both their dates stood them up one evening almost forty years ago and they'd been together ever since. Monae's eyes misted at how damn cute their story was, especially after finding out their Turks and Caicos trip was to celebrate Bertha's two-year remission from breast cancer.

"We're boring by comparison," Marianne said. "Luther and I sat in the cubicles next to each other at the insurance where we work. Our friendship developed pretty slowly and then at our company's Christmas party we realized there was something there. The rest, as they say, is history."

The love shining in her eyes was blinding as she reached forward and kissed her husband.

"That's so cute," Monae gushed, wondering how a brewery tour managed to turn into something that was hitting her with the sweetest feels.

"Your turn," the bartender said. "How did you guys get together?"

Monae froze but Hudson started talking before the silence became awkward. "We're not actually together." He smiled at her. "But the vacation is still young."

"You guys met on the island?" Luther asked.

Hudson shook his head. "No. We're supposed to be on a blind date."

"A blind date?" Luther asked, his eyes going wide. "Nah. Let me buy a round because *this* sounds like a story."

It did make for a hilarious ass story now they were on the other side of it. Everyone around the bar was captivated as Hudson explained and *exaggerated* how ruthless Monae had been in turning down Tempest's attempts to set them up before her wild ass best friend took matters into her own hands.

"They booked us on different airlines on purpose even though we didn't even know what each other looked like," Monae said.

"And she waited until I was already in departure at Miami before she says *don't get mad.*"

"That is at once the most fucked up thing I've ever heard but then also the sweetest," Samantha commented.

Monae sipped her beer and smiled. "I'll accept that their heart was somehow in the right place."

"So were her instincts it seems," Bertha piped up, putting a handful of popcorn in her mouth. "Y'all look like you fit, indeed."

Monae's cheeks went hot at the chorus of affirmative responses to Bertha's observation. She snuck a look at Hudson and found him with a smile teasing his lips. "We'll never hear the end of it if Tempest turns out to be right. That's why Monae decided I definitely don't stand a chance now."

She smacked Hudson playfully. "Don't throw me under the bus like you hadn't been saying the same thing."

He held her hands and brought them to his chest. "Yeah, but that was before."

"Before what?" Monae raised her eyebrow.

Hudson leaned into her again and whispered, "Before I knew how good your body feels against mine."

Monae couldn't find the words to respond to him, not with the way her heart started thumping against her chest. She didn't have to. Bertha's loud chuckle pulled her attention away from the fact Hudson's hand was resting casually on her thigh.

"I might be getting up there in age, but my eyes are working just fine. You say you won't hear the end of it if this friend of yours turns out to be right? Well, I hope y'alls ears are ready to hear her yammer on and on because that woman is right as hell."

CHAPTER TEN

Tension popped up between Hudson and Monae after that little exchange during the brewery tour and it still persisted even as they grabbed cocktails at the hotel's swim up bar later that afternoon. But it was the best kind of tension. She was still struggling with whether she wanted to explore what everyone else saw between them, what he *knew* she felt between them and wanting to stand her ground but he could feel her resolve slipping. It was in how she didn't shy away from his eyes greedily roving over her when she showed up to the pool in an orange one piece that showed off every single curve as if it was painted on her body. It was in the way her touches lingered longer than they ever had before as they joked around while they sipped on cocktails in the refreshing water. Encouraged by her responses, Hudson grabbed a seat on one of the underwater bar stools and held Monae's waist, pulling her gently to sit on his lap. She relaxed against him and continued the stories she'd been telling him about how every single Valentine's Day she could remember sucked. She had already told him about the time her long-term boyfriend started vomiting uncontrollably during their dinner at a fancy restaurant only for it to end up being him having appendicitis and so she had to rush him to the hospital for emergency surgery. Then there was the time she found out she was the side-chick when the man she thought was her boyfriend proposed to his girlfriend on live TV during some local news station's Valentine's Day special. He'd needed to refill their drinks after *that* story. While they sipped on their fresh drinks, Monae started telling him about a disastrous secret Valentine's mishap in middle school. Monae had been excited when she received a secret Valentine's card from someone asking to meet behind the school after the final bell. She was even more ecstatic when she went to the appointed meeting place to find a classmate, Jimmy, who she'd been crushing on all year. It turned out the persons delivering the card had been a little too eager and didn't realize Jimmy had requested his card go to the most popular girl in their class, Monica, and the embarrassed boy had to explain to an equally embarrassed Monae about the mix up.

"Let me tell you," she said through tears of laughter. "My ass didn't know shame until that moment. I almost chose to pass away."

Hudson took a sip of his rum and Coke. "Not gon' lie, that was brutal. You should've been able to sue those kids for emotional distress or something."

"I know right," she giggled before shifting on his lap so she could face him. He went rock hard instantly. Her eyes widened slightly but Hudson shrugged. "I'm only human. I know you know you look hot as hell in that suit."

She chuckled. "That's why I bought it."

"Hey," he said finally remembering to ask the question that kept slipping his mind since he listened in on her video call with Tempest. "Why do they call you Whip?"

Her bright smile stole his breath as she hopped down off him. He only had a few seconds to miss the feel of her body on his before he was caught up with her starting to sing Silentó's 'Watch Me' loudly while she performed the 'Whip and Nae Nae' in the thigh level waters. He couldn't stop laughing, the nickname suddenly making a lot of sense.

"I tried to fight them every step of the way," she laughed. "But you know how stubborn Tempest and Wynn can be. Suddenly everyone in our friend group stopped calling me Nae Nae and started calling me Whip instead."

"I like Nae Nae," he said. "Whip is a really clever play on the name, though."

"I'll give it to her," Monae said. "Tempest is a clever bitch."

She chuckled as she met his gaze and Hudson wondered whether she was thinking about the nickname or if she was thinking about the situation her best friend engineered.

Hudson expected her to grab the bar stool next to his, but she slid back on his lap like she belonged there. He rested his hand loosely at her hip even though he was aching to pull her closer. He didn't want to do anything that might impact the comfortableness settling between them so Hudson decided it was best to just bide his time. He tried to ignore the way his body reacted to having her so close to him that he could feel every breath she took. He pushed away the desire to place light kisses along her shoulder before tipping her chin toward him so he could claim her mouth. And what a mouth that was! They continued chatting, swimming and drinking cocktails until Monae announced she was tired and wanted to order in dinner before she went to sleep. He wondered if she was really that tired or if she needed to put some distance between them. Hudson didn't fight it. He walked her, despite her protests, to her room and brushed his lips lightly against her cheek instead of pulling her into a goodbye hug like he usually did.

"Have a good night, Nae Nae," he whispered as she started making her way into her room. Her mouth opened as if she was going to say something but she snapped it shut almost immediately.

"You too," she said eventually.

"I'll see you tomorrow?" he asked, wanting her to know she still controlled how much they would see each other during the trip.

"Of course," she grinned. "The beaches won't explore themselves. Besides, you're a whole professional photographer. I can't pass up the opportunity to have you make art out of me."

He was cradling her cheek before he could think about it. "Make art out of you? You're already a masterpiece."

Her grin widened. "Flattery will get you everywhere."

"Everywhere?" he asked not bothering to hide the innuendo in his voice. Her soft laughter filled the air between them. "Goodnight, Hudson. See you tomorrow."

He waited until she was safely in her room before he started walking to the elevator with excitement coursing through him. A plan had started forming in his mind as he listened to Monae talk about her terrible Valentine's Days in the past and it was time to head to the concierge's desk to see what he needed to do to make his ideas a reality. Monae had no idea what the next day was about to bring.

CHAPTER ELEVEN

"Room service."

Monae twisted in bed before opening one eye to look at the clock on the bedside table. 6:30 AM. The knocking outside her door continued with the person on the other side announcing he was there with room service even though Monae knew for sure she hadn't ordered any. She pulled the covers over her head and tried to drift back to sleep. She hoped the person would get the hint and realize he mixed up rooms, but the knocking persisted. Monae got out of bed with a groan and pulled on a fluffy, white robe before she trudged to the door, swung it open and started getting ready to tell the person on the other side that he was in the wrong place.

"Monae Alexander?" the woman standing next to the man holding a colorful bouquet asked.

She nodded, growing more confused by the second. The petite woman with deep brown skin and a cute twist out smiled and handed her the flowers. "These are yours. If you'll just let us in, we'll get started with setting breakfast up on the balcony as was requested."

She'd been observing how beautifully the red chrysanthemums

complimented the sunflowers and orange tulips while calla lilies and baby's breath softened the arrangement when the woman's words pulled her up short. *As was requested.*

"I didn't order room service," she said.

"We know," the man, who'd been silent until then, piped up. "It was ordered for you. Can we come set up?"

She stepped aside and they moved with the trays of food to the balcony while she sat on her bed staring at the beautiful flowers as confusion gave way to clarity. Monae grabbed her phone and connected to Hudson's room.

"The flowers are beautiful," she said when his deep voice answered the call.

"Flowers?" he asked. "You got an admirer or something?"

Monae laughed. "Stop messing around. I know you sent them... and breakfast too."

His voice softened. "Guilty. I hope they're setting up your food the way I told them to."

She glanced to the balcony and smiled. "I think so. Thank you. It was a sweet surprise once I stopped being confused. What's the occasion?"

This time he was the one who laughed. "It's Valentine's Day, Nae Nae. I decided to give Russ and Tempest's wallets a break for a day so I could use my own resources to make sure this is the best Valentine's Day you've ever had."

Monae's heart went incredibly soft. She was lost for words. She hadn't been doing anything the day before when she was giving Hudson a rundown of her horrendous Valentine's Day experiences other than make conversation. The horror stories were more humorous than anything now since so much time had passed. She'd never expected him to care enough to go out of his way to make this day a good one. She didn't know what to do with the tender feelings coursing through her so she hid behind humor. "The bar is dirt low."

He laughed. Monae imagined how his eyes crinkled at the

corners while he grinned and suddenly tenderness wasn't the only thing coursing through her body.

"It's a good thing I'm an overachiever," he said. "Make sure they remember to give you your itinerary for the rest of the day."

"My what?"

"Enjoy your breakfast, Nae Nae," he said in a voice that suggested he knew she'd heard exactly what he said. "I'll see you a bit later."

Monae sat on her bed for a few minutes after he disconnected the call before she made her way to the balcony where the breakfast spread was complete. It was a standard fare of croissants, scrambled eggs, bacon, smoked salmon and potato hash but it was the fruit bowl that stopped her in her tracks. Monae was very particular about the fruit she enjoyed. She hated melons and any hint of cantaloupes, honeydews, watermelons or the like turned her completely off. She was forever turning her nose up at fruit bowls for melon contamination since everybody loved to put them into their fruit bowls. She'd wondered if Hudson called Tempest for information about her when she saw the fruit bowl consisted of berries, grapes and pineapple and apple slices but thought it was super random detail to seek out. She was settled around the table when she remembered she'd joined him for breakfast the day before and prepared her own fruit bowl just the way she liked it.

She couldn't wipe the grin off her face as she popped a grape into her mouth and took a sip of the champagne that had been poured. The woman handed her an envelope before she and her coworker left Monae to enjoy her breakfast. She laughed long and hard when she opened the envelope and pulled out the note, which was headed: *Monae's Best Valentine's Day*.

God, he was sweet and thoughtful as hell. She kept chuckling as she moved through the list. He wasn't lying when he said he was an overachiever. He had her scheduled for an hour-long massage and facial at the hotel's spa, followed by a request she put on her favorite bikini for something they were apparently going to be doing from 11:00 AM and then at 7:00 PM he scribbled 'Fancy feat Monae Alexander' which she assumed was him telling her to dress up.

She spent a relaxing forty-five minutes sipping on champagne and eating her breakfast as she looked out at the strikingly beautiful ocean. She'd barely finished her last bite before she did what she was dying to do.

Tempest answered on the second ring. She was about to start rambling about how sweet Hudson was when Tempest's face pulled her up short.

"You okay?" she asked, her elation immediately being replaced with worry for her friend. Tempest made a hand motion brushing Monae's question off as if she didn't look like death warmed over.

"This kid be on some bullshit every morning," Tempest said. "...and afternoon and evening. I'm so exhausted."

A small smile spread across her lips. "Why are *you* calling me looking so damn excited at this early hour, though? You let him hit it, didn't you?"

"I guess the kid could be on a little bit more bullshit if you're finding time to tease me like that," Monae said dryly. "But no. I didn't let him hit it..."

Her voice trailed off and Tempest's loud cackle rang out from the phone. "But you want to. It's okay, Whip. You can admit I was right about him."

"It's not even that he's funny and sexy, good company and sexy, talented and sexy," Monae giggled. "He's a damned sweetheart too. Do you know what he did?"

Monae gave her a quick rundown of their visit to the brewery followed by everything leading up to Hudson promising to make today her best Valentine's Day ever... and well... already succeeding.

"I love the way he was quick to let you know me and Russ weren't paying for anything he was doing for you today," Tempest laughed. "But what can I say? Somebody raised those Bradley men right."

"For damn sure," Monae laughed.

"Whip, I'm sorry for how I forced you guys together. I know the end doesn't always justify the means, but I feel just as strongly as I did a few months ago," her friend said. All the humor was gone from her voice when she continued, "What are you going to do now? Are you going to forgive me and Russ for the shit we were on and lean into whatever could happen between you and Hudson?"

"Did you hear he picked up on my stupid melon thing just by observation? Did I show you the bouquet? Have you seen his ass?" Monae asked. "Lean? Temp, you can just go 'head and call me the Tower of Pisa."

CHAPTER TWELVE

It was the smile for him.

Monae's smile was wide and relaxed as she walked towards him right when they'd agreed to meet. Her hair fell around her shoulders and she'd painted her lips with bright red lipstick. She wore a black, sheer maxi dress to cover the red bikini she was wearing with dainty black sandals on her feet. Damn. He'd promised himself today would be all about Monae and that he'd keep his hands to himself, but he wasn't sure he would be able to make good on that promise. Especially when she walked up to him, rose to her toes and planted a soft, shy kiss on his lips that seemed to shock her as much as it shocked him. He resisted the urge to pull her back in so he could taste her properly.

"What did I do to deserve that?"

"Thank you for this morning," she said. "It was perfect."

"I hope the rest of the day goes just as well," he said, extending his hand to her. She slid her hand into his and glanced up at him. "Even if everything is disaster after this you've already won the best Valentine's Day aim."

"Aye, don't jinx this," he grinned squeezing her hand. "I want all of this to be perfect for you."

"Why would you go through all of this trouble?" she asked as he helped her into the taxi the company he'd planned the catamaran cruise they were about to take with had sent.

"Because you deserve it."

She rolled her eyes as she slid into the back of the luxury sedan. "You don't even know me like that to be able to make such a bold ass statement."

Hudson wanted to kiss the skepticism from her lips but instead he turned so he could look her straight in the eyes. He ran his thumb across her jaw line. "You're right, I don't actually know you that much yet. But it feels like I do."

"You're really good with the flattery," Monae said in a soft voice.

"I'm not trying to flatter you," he said. "If anything, I'm afraid saying these kinds of things will send you running. But every word I speak is true."

Her lips quivered slightly as she said, "I'm still here."

Hudson couldn't help himself. To hell with waiting. He tipped her chin towards him and claimed her mouth, his entire body setting ablaze when she sighed a little, allowing him to slip his tongue inside. His hands found the back of her head, pulling her into him as he angled his mouth so he could kiss her more deeply. About fucking time. Her lips felt like heaven against his and Hudson hardened when she moaned and started sucking on his tongue. She was halfway to straddling him in the back seat when the driver's cough slashed through the haze of lust that filled the air like they'd been smoking a joint back there. Hell, the effect was pretty much the same. His head was light, heart thumping and body felt like it would drift away if not for the part of his anatomy that was heavy, straining and desperate to find comfort in Monae's warmth. He'd expected her to jump away from him once the driver tried to get their attention, but she didn't. She kissed him slowly and deeply for a few more seconds before she eased herself back down on the seat and adjusted her cover up.

He couldn't stop looking at her. Not when her eyes sparkled with promises of more and the way her heaving chest drew attention to her breasts barely restrained by her bikini top. He brushed a few pieces of her hair from her face and planted a quick kiss on the side of her head before he pulled together the few pieces of coherent thoughts left in his head and turned to the driver.

"Sorry for the interruption," the man said, not even trying to hide his amusement with the whole situation. "I just wanted to introduce myself. I'm Bev and I'm here to see to it you get to your catamaran for your private charter safely. If you have any questions or you have any suggestions for what you want me to play for the quick ride over let me know, but I think I've got the perfect song to fit the mood."

He chuckled again before he put the car into gear and started easing it out from where it'd been parked. He was fiddling with his phone for a bit and Hudson nearly passed out with laughter when the sounds of music filled the car. Hudson looked over to see Monae wiping amused tears from her face and Bev was barely holding it together when he caught the man's eyes in the rearview mirror.

"I've got the perfect song to fit the mood," Bev had said and then he put on Beyoncé's 'Partition'.

Well played, Hudson thought. *Well played.*

CHAPTER THIRTEEN

Hudson hadn't been joking when he said he'd gone all out. She'd suspected from the timetable he'd sent at breakfast that they would be doing something involving the water but she hadn't expected him to charter a catamaran. They had to walk a short distance from the car along the beach towards where the catamaran had been moored close to the shore. Hudson kept a possessive hand on her lower back and he held her shoes as she waded through the shallow waters to get to the stairs leading up on to the boat. A smiling woman with dark skin and box braids flowing down her back greeted them and led them to a small sitting area with a table filled with chocolate covered strawberries and a bottle of champagne on ice. She slid into the L-shaped area and leaned back against the red cushions with a smile. The sun was high in the sky, casting soothing rays against her skin while turquoise waters stretched out before them. Chilled reggae played through the speakers and the champagne was cold and bubbly against her lips. This was nice. It was beyond nice. She couldn't believe this man had taken it upon himself to plan and execute such a gorgeous day for her without any sort of encouragement. Monae felt like she was in some alternate Universe. She'd started believing men like this didn't actually exist.

"You like it?" Hudson asked, tipping his champagne flute against hers before taking a sip.

"How could I not? This is beautiful."

The hostess, Ellen, informed them that they were going to be sailing to a good spot to get some snorkeling done before they brought out the lunch spread.

"You don't have to if you don't want," Hudson laughed. He gestured to her hair. "I know I didn't leave a lot of time on the schedule between this and dinner. Even though you'll be drop dead gorgeous no matter what, just know I won't feel any type of way if you choose your hair being *laid* laid over snorkeling around some old ass shipwreck or whatever Ellen said."

He was grinning in a way Monae could only describe as cute and she let relief surge through her. She would've taken that as a sly suggestion to sit out the snorkeling if it had come from her ex, but she could hear the genuineness in Hudson's voice. Monae smacked his shoulder playfully and said, "Like I'm going to pass up anything on offer today."

Hudson raised an eyebrow as he pulled his lips through his teeth. "Anything, huh?"

A coy response rose to her lips but Monae bit it back. She almost climbed him in the back of the sedan... the coyness stage was about three miles behind them. She picked up a strawberry and brought it to her mouth. She wrapped her lips around it in slow, purposeful movements and sucked gently before she sank her teeth into it. She licked away the stray bits of chocolate before she said, "Anything."

He squeezed his eyes shut and groaned. "I didn't pin you as being wicked."

Monae chuckled, shifting her position so she could throw one leg over him. "Me? Wicked? Never."

"Don't tease me with something we can't act on right now."

Her lips parted in exaggerated surprise. "What do you mean we can't act on it right now?"

His hands went to her waist, pulling her so she could sit on him. Her eyes widened slightly when she felt him pressed against her ass cheek.

He chuckled. "I told you before, Nae Nae, I'm only human."

An above average one, it seemed, if what she felt was anything to go by. She took a few seconds to compose herself before she angled her body so she could look at him. "What do you mean we can't act on it right now?"

She nodded her head towards the middle of the catamaran which had short steps down to where Ellen explained a bathroom, limited seating and a small bedroom was located. "I know there's a bed somewhere down there."

Monae found herself fixating on the way his Adam's apple bobbed up and down when he threw his head back and laughed. Heat rushed to her pussy. Was her body short-circuiting? Why the hell did she find that so sexy?

"Yes," he said, still laughing. "There's a bed somewhere down there but we're not going to use it."

Monae made a face, sticking her bottom lip out and gave him her best impression of a spoiled child being denied something they wanted. This little exchange started off as a joke but Monae couldn't shake the image of Hudson bending her over and fucking her to the motion of the sea. He cuddled her close to him. "Because we have a schedule."

She snuggled into him, comfortable against his chest. Monae rested her chin against his collarbone and said, "When did you pencil in your dick for, Mr. Organized?"

His dick twitched against her ass cheek as if it was just as invested in his answer as she was.

"I didn't pencil my dick in. Today wasn't supposed to be about any of that. I just wanted you to have a good time," he said. "But... if I had thought about penciling it in, our first time wouldn't be below deck on some cramped catamaran where you wouldn't even be able to scream how you're gonna need to."

The quiet confidence in that statement sent excited tingles down Monae's spine. "Oh? So, it's like that?" she asked, not even caring that her voice was sounding a bit breathless. He pressed his lips to hers. "And more."

CHAPTER FOURTEEN

Hudson was grateful Russ convinced him to pack a dinner suit by telling him he had at least one posh restaurant on their itinerary and he wanted them to fit in. He chuckled as he shrugged into his black tuxedo jacket. Russ and Tempest really thought this scam through... well except for the insanity of the plan in the first place. Hudson wasn't thinking of the plan as insane when he meandered to the lobby where he collected the bouquet of roses the concierge sourced and had ready for him. His mind was stuck on Monae. They spent nearly six hours together and Hudson still wondered how they didn't succumb to the attraction hanging thickly in the air between them. He wondered if he was crazy for not dragging her to the bed below deck so he could savor her every time he stole a kiss or felt her warm, soft skin beneath his palms when he cuddled her to him. When she finally pulled off the coverup to reveal the tiny ass red bikini she wore, Hudson *knew* he was crazy for trying to resist her. He spent the entire cruise in a state of heightened arousal. His blood burned hot every time she rocked her hips to the playlist filled with upbeat reggae, dancehall and R&B tunes that Ellen had made for them. She'd tossed her hair over her shoulder and smiled wickedly at him when Aaliyah's 'Rock the Boat' started up. He should've seen the mischief in her eyes or even in the way those full lips curved upwards, but he'd been too distracted by her ass. It was his own damn fault he hadn't been prepared for her sashaying over to where he sat and straddling him, seductively rolling her hips and grinding against his crotch as she mouthed Aaliyah's words. That rocked his self-control harder than Aaliyah wanted her lover to rock the boat, but he managed to pull through... barely. If Monae had rocked against him just a little longer she would've had something to roast him about in her group chat, which he was sure would get back to Russ who would clown the fuck out of him. The persistent hard on aside, Hudson couldn't have asked for a better day. It was more than the sunshine, gentle lapping of the ocean or the colorful schools of fish that circled the shipwreck he and Monae explored before lunch. It was more than Monae indulging him and his camera for nearly half an hour as he took shots of her. The camera loved Monae just as he'd predicted when she first stormed into the sushi restaurant what felt like ages ago. It was in the way everything seemed effortless and easy with her. He didn't feel any pressure to impress her with stories of his accomplishments in photography. She listened to him talk excitedly about his photo gallery and offered small bits of legal advice he hadn't considered. He didn't shy away from telling her some of the most embarrassing stories from his childhood, like how he experienced his first wet dream while sleeping over at his best friend's Kyle's house when he was twelve. His regular dorky-assed self was enough and that hit Hudson in places he could barely explain. He and Monae bantered endlessly while they got into playful arguments as they discussed their favorite liquors, fast food restaurants and TV shows. She preferred fruity cocktails to the dark liquor he always found himself imbibing. The Burger King versus McDonalds debate lasted nearly twenty damn minutes with Monae eventually having to concede that McDonalds had the fries game on lock, but he had to admit his preference for a McDonalds burger probably had more to do with fond memories of after school visits with his mother than actual tastiness. They had to agree to disagree on the Family Matters versus French Prince debate since the only things they could agree on were that Urkel was better off with Myra and they preferred the original Aunt Viv.

"Damn," Monae had said, nestling herself into him. "First hating shrimp and actually thinking Fresh Prince is more iconic than Family Matters. I'm starting to wonder if you have any taste at all."

He'd kissed away the smirk from her lips before he said, "Questioning the taste of the man who thinks you're the most beautiful woman to walk this goddamned earth is an interesting take."

Hudson thought Monae was beautiful, but he realized he'd seriously underestimated how enchanting she was as he watched her take in his compliment. Her eyes went soft and the faintest of smiles tugged at her lips.

"You see?" he whispered, dragging his lips across her cheek. "So fucking beautiful."

Hudson had to accept he was still underestimating her beauty when the door to her hotel room swung open and she stepped out to meet him. *Damn*. She pulled her hair into a bun on top of her head and wore minimal makeup except for the burgundy lipstick he couldn't wait to kiss off. And her dress... *wow*... her dress. The black, velvet dress hugged her figure and was sexy as hell even with the high neckline and long sleeves. Then she turned around and Hudson forgot to breathe. The dress had no back. It came down so low he could see the dimples in her lower back where he imagined his thumbs would fit perfectly when he bent her over and finally sated the lust that burned hotter each second. He pushed the hand not holding the bouquet into his pockets to prevent himself from reaching out and tracing a finger up her spine before following it with his tongue.

"Easy, boy," he whispered to himself, well to his dick, when he felt it harden.

Monae tossed a look over her shoulder. "You said something?"

He embraced her from behind, his hand coming to rest on her hip as he handed her the bouquet and kissed the side of her head. "Nothing you need to hear."

She chuckled, brought the roses to her nose and sniffed before turning her neck and tilting it upwards so she could kiss him. "Beautiful."

"Yes, you are," he whispered against her cheek, unable to stop his fingers from digging into her hips as he dropped his lips to her neck and kissed her there until she was arching into him. He ran his hand upwards, cupping her left breast through the fabric and circling with his thumb until he could feel her nipple harden under his touch. He grasped the hardened nub as best as he could between his fingers and squeezed, squeezing a bit harder when she made a startled sound in her throat while he ran his tongue along her earlobe. His dick throbbed hard, begging Hudson to put it out of its misery. Hudson's heart thudded against his chest. The taxi was downstairs waiting and the reservations were made but he couldn't help but wonder how long it would take to ease her out of that dress and bury his face between her legs. He'd gladly spend the rest of the night being uncomfortably hard in his pants if he could have the pleasure of her taste on his tongue. She shivered when he sunk his teeth into her earlobe and Hudson almost took her keycard to let them into her room but reason prevailed. Just barely. His nostrils flared as he tried to regain control when Monae ground her ass against him once he started putting some space between them. He spun her around to face him and smiled when he saw how dazed and unfocused her gaze was.

"We're going to be late," he said. "The reservation is for eight."

"I'm not hungry," Monae shot back. "At least not for anything we can get at that restaurant."

She stepped back into his arms and it took every bit of Hudson's willpower to resist the offer she was putting on the table.

"It'll be a quick dinner," he promised. "You're looking too damn beautiful not to show off."

Monae opened her mouth to argue with his assertion but he smiled at her. "Besides, babe. We're gonna need the energy."

CHAPTER FIFTEEN

The restaurant was gorgeous with outdoor seating in a tropical garden and twinkling lights wrapped around the base of coconut trees. The breezes coming off the nearby beach fluttered across Monae's exposed back and were cool enough for her to pretend her hardened nipples were down to the air instead of the steady beat of arousal that coursed through her as if it had taken on a life of its own. She squeezed her legs together, for the millionth time, but her pussy still throbbed. Hudson wasn't playing fairly. He showed up to her room looking like a god in his black tuxedo that seemed tailor made to his body. She couldn't stop the small sigh that escaped when he turned to lead her to the elevator and she noticed, for the first time, just how powerful his legs were and how his pants molded against the tight ass she couldn't wait to sink her nails into as he thrust into her. He smelled like something spicy and woodsy and Monae's stomach tightened whenever she caught a whiff of him. But by far the biggest indication that Hudson had no damn intention to play fair was the pair of black-rimmed, square shaped glasses that donned his face. He'd been wearing contacts for the last couple days, denying Monae the absolute sex on legs he became with the addition of something as simple as glasses. Tempest had called him Monae-kryptonite and she was damn right. She was still wound tight with the memories of being pressed against him as his hands roamed all over her body. Damn Hudson for giving her the closest taste of what being with him, *actually being with him*, would be like and then not giving her the satisfaction of cumming all over him. But she would. It was inevitable at this point. She wished she could pay better attention to the restaurant's ambience, the elite service, tasty food and perfectly made cocktails, but she couldn't. It was hard to appreciate how the lobster melted on her tongue like butter when she was busy wondering how Hudson's dick would feel in her mouth. It was hard to concentrate on the conversation they were having about Hudson's first celebrity job when she couldn't stop looking at the way his lips formed the words and imagining them all over her body. It was hard to concentrate on the various smells wafting from the kitchen and the ocean breeze when Monae was so damned wet she worried the scent of her arousal clung to the air around them. She pressed herself down in her chair as if it would soothe her, but it didn't do shit. Monae was seriously contemplating stealing off to the restroom for a few minutes to take the edge off but she knew that would be giving her an unfair advantage. It wasn't like Hudson wasn't *obviously* suffering too. His eyes were fixated on the small rises in her dress where her hardened nipples poked against velvet, his stiff posture was at odds with the engaging, funny conversation he was carrying on and every so often Monae caught him looking at her with so much unrestrained need that she wondered if she'd be able to handle him.

We're gonna need the energy, he'd said, and it was all Monae could think about as she ate her lobster linguini and sipped her strawberry margarita. If Hudson fucked with half the intensity that he devoted to anything else, she would need the energy indeed.

Monae squeezed her thighs together, harder this time, as she pushed another fork filled with food into her mouth. She couldn't wait.

CHAPTER SIXTEEN

The restaurant was gorgeous but everything was wasted on Hudson. He felt like he was sitting in Dante's second circle of hell, ravished by lust for the woman who sat across from him looking better than anyone had any right to. He'd had her in his arms just over two hours before – soft, pliant and wanting him – and he'd put off satisfying his need for her... *again*. He regretted the choice soon after he made it and then spent the rest of the night cursing himself for being an idiot. His intentions might have been noble, but nobility wasn't enough to soothe the torture when he was so hard his pants tented under the table. Especially, when he caught Monae looking at him like she wished he had listened to her and they'd skipped dinner altogether. He'd ordered mashed potatoes with a steak which was cooked perfectly medium rare, but it could have been cardboard in his mouth for how much he appreciated it. Hudson's review of the restaurant would probably be '*great place, would recommend but advisable not to come when you are about to combust with horniness and the object of your lust is sitting near you*'. He'd brought his camera to capture some shots of the restaurant but Hudson found himself obsessed with taking quick, candid portraits of Monae, bathed in the soft light. God, she was beautiful.

"How was your meal?"

The server startled Hudson because he had been busy trying to immortalize each angle of Monae's face in his mind.

"It was great," she said with a small smile. "I enjoyed the cocktail too."

"The steak was amazing," Hudson chipped in as the woman leaned forward and started clearing the empty plates.

"Dessert?" she asked. "The specials for tonight are a four layered chocolate cake and tiramisu."

His eyes met Monae's who was shaking her head ever so slightly.

"Don't you dare," she mouthed.

Hudson smiled. "Perhaps one of each to go?"

The server glanced between them with amusement before she chuckled. "I got you."

Monae took a deep drink from her cocktail, licking some of the excess drink from her lips and Hudson was surprised to find his dick could get harder. He reached out and enveloped her hand in his, running his finger over the ring she wore on her middle finger. Very soon Hudson wouldn't have to wonder what Monae's face would look like when she couldn't contain the pleasure she felt. He'd have a front row seat, and that was worth the motherfucking wait.

CHAPTER SEVENTEEN

The snug fit of the black, velvet dress she'd paired with red stilettos got the desired effect from Hudson when she'd stepped out of her hotel room and his eyes darkened with lust. However, the snugness paired with the length of the dress was just damn inconvenient now that she and Hudson were in the back of the taxi and she ached to feel his hands on more than her bare back. His fingertips seemed to be infused with lightning for how each line he traced up her spine felt like literal jolts of energy throughout her body. His lips burned a trail of need along her cheek and jaw until she threw her head back to grant him better access to the hollow of her neck. Her stomach tightened and unfurled so rapidly with desire her head spun when he grasped her flesh between his teeth and bit gently. Monae couldn't imagine a single thing in existence that she needed more than Hudson. Not one damn thing. She pressed her lips against his, running her tongue along the inseam of his lips as her hand came to his chest, deepening the kiss when he opened his mouth to let her in. Monae kissed Hudson like the answer to the Universe lay within his mouth. It didn't matter how much she took... she wanted more. And more. And more. His hands busied themselves trying to unravel her hair from the tight ass bun she'd pulled it into. Just thinking about him being so desperate to get closer to her that he resorted to taking her hair down made her pussy throb. Monae groaned when her hair finally came down. Hudson dug his fingertips into her scalp and massaged as his tongue explored her mouth in ways that put her at risk of cumming right there. *Damn.* This was some next level shit and neither Monae nor her body had been prepared.

"You're killing me here," Hudson murmured through an open-mouthed kiss. Monae's hands trailed down his chest towards the erection straining against his pants.

"I guess we both 'bout to die, then," she said, returning her lips to his.

Hudson sank his teeth into her bottom lip before he pulled away, panting slightly when he said, "I can't think of a better way to go."

CHAPTER EIGHTEEN

Hudson tipped the taxi driver extra. The man was the real MVP for ignoring everything going on in the back of his taxi, not to mention he was probably going to find a few hairpins Hudson hadn't managed to pick up after he basically ripped Monae's bun down. His dick was still throbbing and heavy by the time he and Monae somehow managed to get themselves into an elevator. He pressed her against the elevator, barely able to pull his lips from hers long enough to press the button for his floor. Hudson wouldn't call their kisses passionate, fiery or even intense. They were hungry, borne out of a desperation that could only be likened to starvation. He kissed Monae like he hadn't been nourished in years. And perhaps he hadn't. Hudson couldn't remember how any other woman's lips felt against his, he couldn't remember the feel of any other ass under his palm and he definitely couldn't remember ever feeling so crazed. His need for Monae flowed through his blood like poison and her body held the only antidote. He pulled away from her and was barely able to catch his breath as he watched her stare up at him, nostrils slightly flaring, eyes glassy and lips bruised from his kisses. Hudson trailed his fingers down her back before pressing his forehead to hers as he captured her mouth again. He tugged her lips into his mouth – slowly and softly – with the tenderness that swam alongside the heavy current of lust threatening to pull him under. Time itself slowed down when Monae sighed, digging her fingers into his shoulders as she melted into the kiss. They yanked away from each other, but laughed when they realized the sound that startled them was only the elevator chiming to indicate they finally made it to his floor. His heart hammered against his chest when he held his hand out to Monae and she took it with a smile. He stood at the crossroads between lust, anticipation and the sudden fear that there'd be no going back once he crossed this line with Monae. That no other woman could possibly do it for him like she did. Hudson pushed those thoughts away. They were useless, anyway. He would gladly walk barefoot across burning coals than continue denying himself the pleasure of Monae's body. He expected he'd have been all over her as soon as they made it into his room, but he surprised himself by heading to the mini bar instead. He needed to slow this shit down, take the edge off and regain some semblance of control.

Hudson shrugged out of his jacket and tossed it over the armchair in the corner of the room.

"Let me get you something to drink," he said.

He expected Monae to resist but she didn't. She nodded, absentmindedly reaching to the back of her dress. He stood there, like a statue, as she fumbled with the buttons at the back of her neck knowing he wouldn't be able to make himself move – wouldn't be able to tear his eyes away from her – even if his life depended on it. His breath caught in his throat when she started to ease the dress down her body, slowly and provocatively, until it fell into a heap on the floor.

Jesus Christ.

Monae's silhouette in the room's low lighting made his mouth dry; titties sitting high, waist snatched, hips... *fuck*. Hudson took a deep breath and exhaled slowly through his mouth, doubling down on his decision to give his mind and his body some time to get it together.

"About that drink..." he said, finally making himself move to the fridge next to the mini bar. He pulled out a bottle of champagne and placed it on the counter beside the two flutes already resting nearby.

Monae's laughter was breathy with a musical cadence around the edges. Hudson's stomach tightened. Damn it. Everything about this woman turned him on in ridiculously embarrassingly ways. He groaned when Monae came up behind him, pressed herself into his back and brought her hands to his waist, undoing his buttons and unzipping his pants. She slid her hand into his pants, cupped his dick and gave it a little squeeze before she started stroking him as much as the confines of his pants would allow. Hudson shut his eyes and focused on his breathing, desperate to not start moaning before he even had a feel of her pussy. He refused to go out like that.

"About that drink?" Monae teased, without breaking the rhythm she'd fallen into.

"You're being a little... distracting right now," he said. Her laughter vibrated against his back as she took her sweet time removing her hand from his pants and stepping back from him. His body protested the removal of her touch instantly even though Hudson refused to accept that that was why his hands shook a little as he tried to pour the champagne. The lighting was dim, but he could see the amused smile on her face when he handed her a flute. She swirled the amber liquid around for a few seconds before she took a sip. "I didn't expect an intermission."

He took a sip of champagne before leaning forward and kissing her lightly, enjoying the sensation of the bubbles dancing on their lips.

"It was necessary as fuck, though," he said. "I needed to guarantee the... longevity of the show."

Monae threw her head back and laughed. "Scared of this pussy, huh?"

"You've got a lot of talk for somebody who's standing over there wetter than the Niagara Falls."

"Nigga please," she said, laughing hard before she took another sip of champagne.

"Did I lie?" Hudson shot back, his voice deepening as he took a long stride that had him right up in her personal space before he pushed his hand between her legs finding her just as wet as he predicted. His thumb made lazy circles against her clit as he slid a finger inside her, enjoying her soft gasp as he stroked her slowly for a few seconds before he withdrew his finger and brought it to his mouth. He licked away her wetness before he took a gulp of champagne.

"You taste better than the Dom Pérignon," he said, smirking as he brought his hand to her neck. "Pussy pricey."

Whatever response Monae might have had was lost in Hudson crashing his lips against hers as he gently applied pressure to her neck while he deepened the kiss. The feral need returned like a punch to the gut and suddenly Hudson couldn't find it in himself to be worried about a short performance. He needed to touch her, feel her and taste more of her in ways he had never needed anything before. He tried putting the flute on counter, but he misjudged and it fell to the carpet. It took him less than a second to check that it hadn't broken before he hoisted Monae off her feet, fingers sinking into her ass, and carried her to the bed. She looked like a fucking gift spread out on the sheets and Hudson could barely decide where he wanted to put his mouth first. He knew one thing, though, and that was that he wanted to see every inch of her. The dim lighting made for a sensuous view, but it wasn't enough. Hudson wanted to see every beauty spot, every stretch mark, every bit of cellulite, every single mark that all came together to form perfection lying in front of him. He was thankful the hotel, as fancy as it was, had a remote to control the lighting that he'd thrown on the bed before he left earlier that night. He licked his lips when the room brightened and he could finally *see* Monae. *Damn.* This woman wasn't tempting, she was temptation and Hudson was starting to think that where getting a grip was concerned, he and his body already lost the war.

CHAPTER NINETEEN

Monae blinked when the dim lighting was suddenly displaced by vivid brightness. She should have felt at least a bit self-conscious lying under the harsh glare of the light in the middle of the king-size bed with her legs slightly parted. Especially when Hudson's eyes roved over her body with enough hunger that Monae started to feel like a gazelle caught in the cross hairs of a lion. Yet, she didn't feel self-conscious in the slightest. The comfortable familiarity that existed between them from almost the first instant they met continued flowing so easily that instead of feeling shy, Monae brought one hand to her breast and twisted her nipple while the other dove between her legs. She continued playing with her nipple and teased her clit while keeping her gaze trained on Hudson before she slid a finger and then another inside. She moaned when she instantly gushed over her fingers. Hudson hadn't been exaggerating about how wet she was. Niagara Falls, indeed.

"Nae," he breathed but he couldn't seem to decide if he wanted to look at the two fingers sliding in and out of her pussy or the fingers rolling, twisting and tugging her swollen nipple.

"Yes?" she whispered, her breath catching in her throat when he started running his fingers lightly across the skin of her thighs, hips, shoulder and stomach before stopping to grasp the nipple she'd been ignoring. He squeezed gently and then hard enough for a surprised yelp to rush from her mouth. She'd barely had time to adjust to the change in sensation before he leaned forward and captured her nipple between his teeth. He walked the tightrope between pleasure and pain expertly and soon Monae was adding another finger, desperately trying to find the right speed and pressure to maximize friction despite the fact her pussy seemed to be weeping with need for him. She welcomed the intrusion of his tongue when his lips finally returned to her mouth, kissing her until her head swam from the sensation of his tongue against hers, his fingers kneading her breasts and her own fingers trying to pull an orgasm from the pussy that refused to come for her. She couldn't even blame her pussy. Monae got off on her own fingers enough, she was due orgasms caused by the fingers, tongue and dick of the gorgeous man who'd stopped kissing her long enough to start getting undressed. Monae pulled herself up against the headboard so she could fully enjoy watching him strip at the side of the bed. He stopped unbuttoning his shirt and smirked when she brought her fingers to her lips and licked away the absolute mess she'd made.

"Hey," he said, shrugging out of the shirt and letting it fall to the floor. "Save some for me."

She chuckled. "You can get it at the source."

Monae was still laughing at her corny joke when Hudson stopped unbuckling his pants, grasped her legs and dragged her, as she squealed, to the edge of the bed. He was on his knees before she could catch her breath. When he finally settled his mouth between her legs, Monae was sure she would never breathe again. He spread her folds with his tongue and went about the business of lapping and licking at her pussy as if he was really trying to drown himself in her essence. She arched her lower back, pressing herself against his face when his tongue finally found her clit and stroked it with a slow, firm pressure that had her just about ready to jump out her skin. She dug her fingers into the back of his head, pulling him even closer and then wrapped her ankles behind his neck as she ground against his tongue. If he was having any issues breathing, Hudson didn't show it. Monae swore when his big hands palmed her ass before he yanked her into his face and held her in place while he continued the firm flicks against her throbbing clit. Little bolts of pleasure shot through her as her stomach began to tighten. Her legs started shaking but he kept his grip on her ass and kept her in place as he lapped harder against her until she couldn't fight off the pleasure. She came with her legs shaking, hands limp and body twisted up as the nastiest expletives streamed from her lips. Monae expected Hudson to stop the onslaught of his tongue but the reason he was holding her ass with a death grip quickly became apparent. He forced her pussy against his tongue which had to be the damn Energizer Bunny because he kept going. And going. And going. He alternated between licking, sucking and grazing her clit with his teeth until Monae's legs started shaking again.

"Please..." she moaned except she was unclear about what she was asking for. Was she asking him to continue? Did she want him to stop? Monae had no fucking clue about anything beyond feeling like every single nerve ending in her clit was about to implode on itself... again. Her clit throbbed, her pussy throbbed, her *damn asshole* throbbed so intensely that Monae would've been worried about the expensive ass sheets except she doubted she could cum *that* strongly from external stimulation alone. The thought had barely crossed her mind before Hudson was freeing one hand from her ass, still carefully maintaining his grip with the other hand and slid two fingers into her. He stroked her with a hooking motion that brushed right against the spot that was the danger zone. His fingers settled into a rhythm that was quicker and more frantic than the lazy, firm strokes of his tongue and Monae's body couldn't cope. She couldn't decide if Hudson was trying to kill her or perform an exorcism, but the things he was doing with his fingers and tongue were definitely crimes. Felonies, even. The orgasm hit her hard. So damn hard that Monae didn't moan, didn't whimper, didn't scream. She just sobbed silently as her body convulsed while she gushed out her pleasure all over Hudson's face and the bed.

Sorry to those sheets, she thought when she was finally able to form a coherent one. She grinned as she watched Hudson try to wipe the evidence of her orgasm away from his mouth, neck and the top of his chest. He wanted it straight from the source and got a bit more than he bargained for. Her smile faltered slightly when he caught her gaze and held it with an unreadable expression on his face. Was he put off by her body's natural reaction to the pleasure he'd blindsided her with? She cleared her throat and was about to say something when he rose from his knees and pressed his body against hers before running his hands through her hair, pulling her against him for a punishing kiss. He was grinning when he pulled back. "You taste even better straight from the nut."

CHAPTER TWENTY

This can't be my reality, Hudson thought as he finally got around to removing his pants and reached for the condoms he'd picked up from the hotel's gift shop early that afternoon in case they would come in handy. His senses were so full of Monae he could barely think straight. She was so damn overwhelming. Hudson often laughed off the idea of another person possessing the exact type of pheromones liable to drive another out of their damn mind, but he wasn't laughing now. Because what else could explain this? Monae was sexy as hell but he'd been with sexy women before and never reacted as violently as this. His head was foggy like he'd smoked the highest grade while washing it down with overproof rum. His heart was throbbing so hard he hoped this fancy ass hotel had a defibrillator on hand. His legs shook like he was on his last mile of a marathon. Hell, his entire body was shaking, and his dick hadn't come within an inch of her pussy yet. *Damn*. He paused rolling on the condom as panic sliced through him... again. How long was he really going to be able to hold out? He gave himself a little pep talk, reminding himself that there were two things he did exceedingly well: taking bomb ass photographs and slinging his dick. He raised one of Monae's legs to his shoulder, turning to place little kisses along her ankle and then slid into her. And fuck. He took a long drag of air through his mouth, squeezed his eyes shut as his body stilled. He chewed on his lip to prevent the moan lodged in his throat from breaking free. His body was shaking as he tried to rein in the orgasm he was barreling straight towards. He couldn't go out like that. He massaged Monae's breasts and stroked her clit until the urge to cum subsided then he slowly withdrew from her before he thrust in again.

And promptly came.

Stars erupted behind his eyes as his body convulsed with an orgasm that just kept going. He kept his eyes shut until the shaking subsided enough for him to pull out, not wanting to look at Monae. His eyes snapped open when Monae started laughing... loudly.

"Don't start," he warned, but he couldn't help but chuckle too when he looked at her lying there with her hair fanned across the bed, eyes damp and sparkling with amusement. He should be ready to curl himself into a ball of shame but his comfort level with Monae wouldn't allow that. He leaned forward and kissed her until the laughter subsided, but she started again as soon as he pulled his lips away.

He could still hear her laughing when he made a quick run to the bathroom to dispose of the condom. Hudson looked at himself in the bathroom mirror and shook his head. "Really, nigga?"

When he returned to the bed, Monae was wiping away the tears of laughter that streamed down her face.

"Don't even," he said as he reached for her and pulled her into a cuddle.

"Don't what? I warned you that this pussy was magic, but you doubted me," she said with an exaggerated sigh. "At least you learned quick."

"You done?" he asked, raising an eyebrow as he smacked her

ass before kissing her neck. She wriggled into him when he slid a finger into her pussy while he massaged her clit with his thumb.

"Not yet," she said, but her breathing was labored.

"Go 'head then, babe," he encouraged. "Get those jokes in while you still can."

She gasped when he added two more fingers and increased his thumb's pressure against her clit as he started making slow circles.

"You're awfully quiet," he teased nuzzling her neck for a few seconds before he stopped fingering her. His hands went to her hips and squeezed while he turned her on to her stomach. Hudson straddled Monae's ass, careful not to put all his weight on her as he leaned forward and trailed his tongue down her spine. She squirmed under him and his dick was instantly hard against her ass cheeks. He trailed his tongue back up her spine before pulling an earlobe into his mouth and sucking lightly. He wished she'd keep still because her fat ass grinding against his dick was distracting as hell. Monae didn't stop so Hudson decided to lean all the way into it. He placed a small kiss in the middle of her back before he pulled himself into an upright position and spread her ass cheeks so he could rub the entire length of his dick between them. His palm pressed against Monae's lower back, pushing her into the bed as he continued rubbing his length along her pussy and ass until she was squirming and moaning under him. He reached for one of the condoms he'd thrown on the bed and made quick work of sheathing himself. He rubbed the head of his dick against her entrance, dipping it in a little bit before pulling it out again and repeating the action until Monae was trying to throw her ass back at him in earnest but couldn't because he still had her pressed into the bed. He could tease her forever, but his own body was sick of his games. Hudson groaned as he pushed himself to the hilt inside Monae who whimpered as her body stretched to accommodate him. She hadn't been lying, though. Her pussy felt like it was made of magic. He covered her body with his, keeping his thrusts long and slow, circling his hips at the very end of each while he kept her pressed into the bed with the weight of his body. He could feel her pussy clenching and fluttering against him as he kept up the rhythm. Monae alternated between moaning, whimpering and biting the sheets. Keeping the slow, sensuous rhythm was sweet torture when all Hudson wanted to do was fuck Monae with the punishing intensity of the lust that kept his stomach twisted into the tightest knots, but he knew the payoff would be worth it. He continued hitting her with those deep, steady strokes until she was clenching him tighter and those flutters became tremors. She felt so fucking good and this time he could bask in it stroke after stroke.

"You've stopped laughing, huh?" he whispered in her ear. He pulled the soft flesh of her neck between his teeth as he put some more power into his thrusts. Her only response was a deep moan as she gripped the sheets unable to wriggle away from his strokes because of how his weight kept her pressed into the bed.

"Thought so," he murmured with another deep stroke, sucking and nibbling on her earlobe while her moans became more frantic. Hudson was loving the way her body was reacting to him, but he was wise enough to accept that he'd fall over the precipice both he and Monae were at the edge of if he kept it up for much longer. And Hudson was a man with a point to prove. He gave himself a small reprieve by switching up the position, turning her on to her back and pushing her knees towards her chest before he entered her again with one, long stroke. Monae started losing her shit when he finally started fucking her the way he'd been dying to since he'd hugged her after the fish fry two days before. His strokes were hard and fast, drawing guttural groans from deep within his belly while Monae dug her nails into his shoulder as she begged him to keep going *just like that*. The punishing pace wasn't sustainable, not with the way she clenched him, not with how soft and wet she was, not with how damned beautiful she looked with her eyes glassy with desire. And definitely not when she parted those full, sexy lips and screamed that he was going to make her cum. His thrusts faltered but he was able to hang on to his rhythm, just barely, until Monae became a blubbering mess of screams and spasmed against his dick so hard he couldn't hold on to his nut even if he had the will to. Hudson released Monae's legs and collapsed on top of her in a heap trying, but failing, to get his breathing to return to normal. He pressed his forehead to hers, planting soft kisses against her lips when he finally pulled himself together.

"My dick ain't no laughing matter, Nae Nae," he said.

She hit him with a wide smile that he felt right in his chest. "Clearly not. My pussy has instructed me to apologize for my flagrant disrespect. We'll spend as much time as required to make up for it."

CHAPTER TWENTY-ONE

Monae propped herself up on her elbow as she watched Hudson and his sexy ass saunter to the bathroom to clean himself up and sighed. She could've had six months of being fucked like this if she hadn't been so damned stubborn. Imagine that. She knew Hudson was the sexiest man to walk the earth once she discovered his intricate tattoo did, in fact, extend across his shoulder and covered his upper chest and back. She knew he was the most talented man to walk the earth when he kneeled before her and ate her out in ways that should be illegal. Yet, it was the self-deprecating way he handled her teasing him about cumming quickly that solidified for her that she really wanted... no *needed* to see how things could develop between them outside of this island paradise. Though, she supposed, it was easy to not take the teasing to heart when he knew what his 'A' game felt like. She clenched her thighs together as her pussy throbbed pleasantly with the muscle memory of exactly what that dick could do. He was already working with above average material, but Hudson proved how important it was to actually *know* how to use what the Lord blessed him with. She was still lying there with a silly smile on her face when he returned with a warm, wet towel and started wiping between her legs, placing small kisses on the insides of her thighs when he was done. She settled into Hudson's arms with contentment coursing through her veins. Damn, this man was something else. He nuzzled his face into her neck and asked, "So how was your Valentine's Day?"

"Honestly the best I've ever had. Probably the best I'll ever have."

Hudson stopped tracing the small circles he'd been making against her back. "That you'll ever have? We'll see about that."

"You're saying you're going to be around for more Valentine's Days?"

Monae's lust roused to life at the sound of his deep, hearty laughter before he eventually answered her.

"You tell me. Are you still running or should we be looking for thank you gifts for Russ and Temp?"

He'd stopped nuzzling her neck and leaned back so he could look her in her eyes. Monae's heart started beating wildly against her chest as the implications of what Hudson was saying set in.

"You sure you don't want to hold off on that? Vacation Monae and stressed out attorney Monae are two different people."

"Don't do that," Hudson said. The seriousness that crept into his voice surprised Monae. "Do what?"

"Don't downplay what's going on here between us," he said. "I'm not naïve enough to think I've already seen all facets of you, babe. What I *do* know is I can't wait to discover every single one of them, even the ones that might drive me to drink a little."

"But..."

"Nope," he whispered. He dropped a kiss on her forehead, then her nose and finally her lips. "No downplaying. We need to take our asses down to your room so we don't have to sleep on these wet sheets."

"I'm not downplaying anything," she said, feeling the need to let him know he wasn't alone in whatever this topsy-turvy, magical, downright incredible thing between them was. "I've just never had anything that seems so... natural. So easy."

Hudson shrugged. "Neither have I, but you know what? Sometimes a good thing is just a good thing. We could waste time waiting for the other shoe to drop or trying to figure out how an idiot like Russ managed to be right about two things in his life or we could bask in this. Now lemme go find some shorts or something for you to wear so I can smuggle your pretty little ass to your room for us to get some rest."

CHAPTER TWENTY-TWO

"Your stares are loud," Monae whined, her eyes slowly fluttering open. She stretched her hands above her head and tried to stretch out her sleepiness but ended up curling herself deeper into the sheets. Hudson didn't fight the smile tugging at the corners of his lips. "I can't help looking at you."

It was true too. He'd awoken nearly thirty minutes before to find that he and Monae had found separate corners of the bed even though they'd fallen asleep tangled up in each other. She was sleeping with her hands tucked under her chin and knees pulled into her stomach, a position that seemed just as uncomfortable as the one she'd been in during the flight. Her adorable ass was wearing a bright pink bonnet that had started sliding off her head. He wondered if she knew she sucked on her lips as she slept. Hudson wished he'd had his camera but settled on snapping a few photos with his cell phone. He played with the settings and tried to find the angles that did justice to the light streaming into the room. He'd expected her to wake up for all the shuffling he'd been doing but Monae slept on. She didn't wake up until long after he'd put the phone away and got back into the bed, watching her silently as she slept.

"Okay, creep," she laughed, pressing her body into him. Monae dropped a kiss on his shoulder, running her tongue along one of the thick lines of his tattoo before she placed a chaste kiss against his lips. He tried to draw her into a deeper kiss but she pulled away mentioning something about morning breath. Hudson rolled on top of her and blew his breath into her face, holding her in place as she squealed and tried to push him away.

"If you can't love me with my stank breath you don't deserve me with my minty fresh."

Monae howled with laughter. "Boy! If you don't stop messing around."

He pressed a kiss against her cheek. "Is this okay?"

He didn't wait for her to answer but, instead, continued kissing along her jaw, neck and collarbone before trailing his tongue all the way down to her belly button. He made circles there, enjoying the way she laughed and tried to push him off, pleading with him that she was ticklish. He kissed his way straight down to her mound before he raised his head, caught her gaze and said, "I've got a solution to our morning breath problem."

She'd barely managed to ask him what he was talking about before he spread her legs just enough for him to bury his face in her pussy. Her body jerked against him when he started exploring her sex with his tongue. He kissed those lips just the way he'd have kissed her mouth if she'd allowed him to. Hudson was intoxicated by her taste, smell and the way she felt under his tongue. Her little cries had him desperate to drive her to the brink, but he restrained himself. There'd be time for that. He feasted on her until he got his fill and then worked his way back up her body before claiming her mouth. She responded to the kiss by interlinking her hands behind his head and pulling him closer while she wrapped her legs around his waist. They were panting when Hudson finally managed to pull away from the kiss.

"Who needs mouthwash when you're already so sweet?"

CHAPTER TWENTY-THREE

Sometimes a good thing is just a good thing.

Monae tried to hold on to Hudson's words as the small bit of doubt she'd felt the night before reared its ugly head again. Things were easy – *too fucking easy* – between her and Hudson. Yes, sometimes a good thing was just a good thing but that never happened to *her*. Definitely not where relationships were concerned. If someone wrote a documentary about the state of Monae's romantic life it would be called *All Her Life She Had To Fight (And Sis Lost Plenty)*. She used to joke with Tempest and Wynn telling them her road to love was paved with shards of glass dipped in sulfuric acid interspersed with rusty nails. They accused her of being dramatic and maybe she was but that was the way things felt. It felt that way when she spent nearly a year in a relationship with a man who, upon reflection, didn't even like her for just how one-sided the effort was. It felt that way when after licking her wounds for a few months Monae allowed her friend Barbara to set her up on a blind date with her cousin, Ian. That relationship seemed to be going well for about six months or so until Monae had to watch him propose to his girlfriend and mother of the two kids he never mentioned on live TV. She cut

Barbara off just as firmly as she did her idiot cousin and vowed she'd never allow anyone to set her up again. Not that her own choices were much better. Monae pushed aside the bitter feelings memories of Robert always brought up and tried to focus on the reason her feelings were all helter skelter now. Hudson was holding her hand as they browsed souvenir shops in Grace Bay looking way better than anyone had a right to in a white T-Shirt, black shorts and aviator shades. It was so damned easy to be with him. They'd spent most of the morning wrapped up in each other in bed as Hudson continued to turn her out in ways her body wasn't prepared for. Hell, Monae doubted there was any way she could prepare her body for the pleasure that came with making love to Hudson. There definitely wasn't any way she could prepare herself for the tenderness that bloomed in her heart each time they came together. Monae spent almost all her sex life trying to be perfect in bed. She'd flat out refuse to have sex if she wasn't perfectly waxed, often tried to control her moans because she worried she sounded like a wailing goat when she was overwhelmed with pleasure and she shied away from positions that didn't flatter her body. She'd dated Robert for nearly three years, *was engaged to marry him for fuck's sake*, and he'd never had sex with her while she had her bonnet on. She always remembered to remove it and Robert sure as hell remembered on the few occasions she'd been too caught up to think about it. Monae hadn't given her bonnet a single thought as she and Hudson made love that morning and neither had he. She wasn't concerned about her angles, her moans or frankly anything other than how he felt moving inside her. She wasn't paralyzed by shame when she moved too close to the edge of the bed as she tried to climb on top of him and tumbled to the floor.

Hudson leaned over the bed with laughter in his eyes and teased. "I mean if you wanted us to continue on the floor you could've just said so."

The impish smile on his face was enough to get Monae

laughing along with him. Monae was halfway through pulling herself into a sitting position when Hudson climbed down from the bed, leaned his back against the frame while beckoning for her to come straddle him. She gladly obliged. Monae didn't replay her uncoordinated moves in her mind when she sank down on Hudson's thickness and his hands came to her waist, encouraging her to ride him while murmuring about how she was driving him crazy and how good her pussy felt. He looked at her like she was the answer to all his dreams and trailed his hands across her skin like she was made of precious gems. And when they came, they came together with foreheads pressed against each other's as they rode the waves of pleasure. *So damn easy.*

They ordered in food and ate on the balcony cuddled up together, stealing kisses and lazy strokes geared at driving each other crazy until Hudson suggested they at least explored the island a little bit since it was their last full day. Their conversation never stalled because Monae never felt a need to filter anything that came out of her mouth with him. They explored the museum, drove to Chalk Sound to check out the view along the coast, trying to get glimpses of fancy houses, before they finally came back to Grace Bay to check out souvenirs. She posed for photos outside of the white buildings with navy blue trimmings that combined with the interspersed greenery and bright blue skies made the day feel even more like a fairy tale. *So damn easy*. So why was panic making it hard for her to breathe?

"You okay?" Hudson asked, squeezing her hand as they moved to the front of the line in Turkberry, the frozen yogurt shop Hudson had wanted to try out. Monae couldn't see his eyes behind the dark aviators but his forehead was furrowed. She didn't blame him. She had gone a bit quiet over the last twenty minutes. The lie was on the tip of her tongue, but she couldn't bring herself to lie to him.

"I'm feeling overwhelmed by this," she admitted, pointing between them both so he knew she wasn't talking about the assortment of toppings they had to choose from. Monae waited for the rush of panic she would feel with Robert to pop up at the thought of allowing her overthinking to ruin what was on track to being a perfect day.

"Tell me," he said, his voice was soft and filled with concern. She'd started opening her mouth when he brushed his lips against hers. "Maybe after we order our yogurts and find someplace a little more private?"

Monae nodded, accepting the logic in his suggestion. She waited for him to remove his hand from hers, to put some space between them or to start acting cold, but he didn't. If anything, Hudson pulled her closer as she tried to decide on her toppings, teasing her when she overloaded her plain yogurt with every chocolate topping Turkberry had before he ordered a mango yogurt with strawberry slices.

"I didn't expect your order to be so boring," she said while they walked to the back of the establishment to find seating. He flashed her a dimpled smile. "There are five-year-olds who would look at your order and think you were doing too much."

"Shut up," she laughed. "You better not try stealing any of mine."

His smile widened. "Can't make any promises, Nae Nae. You know I don't like keeping my hands to myself."

She blushed wildly when he squeezed her ass before pulling out a bright pink chair for her and sliding into the one opposite hers. Monae was still so engrossed in the light flirting she almost forgot they were about to have a serious conversation. *So damn easy.*

CHAPTER TWENTY-FOUR

They had been having the best day... until they weren't. It wasn't any one thing she did that set Hudson's nerves on edge, but a combination of how she'd gone from being jovial and joking to eerily silent and the way the little absentminded touches he'd started to look forward to abruptly stopped. Monae had disappeared into her head somewhere between them picking up a cute onesie for Russ and Tempest's baby and trying to find a good place to have a late afternoon cool down before heading back to the hotel.

Overwhelmed.

The word was like a dagger straight through his chest even though Hudson tried his best to play it off. The last thing either of them needed was for him to act out because his feelings were hurt and make things more uncomfortable than they needed to be. This wasn't the first time Monae brought up misgivings. The first time he'd tried to silence them with a few optimistic words and a generous serving of dick. He could accept that that was the wrong move as he watched Monae take small bites of her frozen yogurt, her anxiety bouncing off her like sound waves.

"I'm sorry," he said.

Beautiful, hazel eyes widened as her gaze locked on his. "For what?"

"I've come on too strong and I dismissed your feelings last night."

Monae shook her head, reaching across the table to hold his hand. His anxiety levels dropped a little bit.

"This isn't you *at all*," she said. "You're not pushing any harder than I would expect you to. Not if you're feeling the way I'm feeling."

She lowered her eyes and smiled a little before she looked him in the eyes again. "I like you. I *really really* like you and it's just so easy when I'm around you. I know you believe sometimes a good thing is just a good thing and I should chill..."

"And that's exactly what I'm apologizing for," he said. "I'm not that guy and I don't endeavor to ever be the guy who tries to dismiss his woman's feelings because he feels differently. Whatever you're feeling is valid and so I want us to discuss it and try to find a way to hopefully get on whatever page includes us giving this thing a real shot."

The shock that flashed across her pretty face was enough to make Hudson want to back down from inadvertently calling her his woman, but he kept his mouth shut. Because what the fuck else was she if not *his woman*? His soul wouldn't know peace until she was comfortable with that eventuality.

"Are you for real?" she asked with a little shake of her head. "Like, honestly, are you for real or did Tempest put you up to this to teach me a lesson?"

Hudson jerked his head back. He would've been amused by the question if Monae didn't look kind of, well, serious.

"Run that by me again but do it real slow like I'm a toddler or something," he said.

She shoved some of her yogurt into her mouth in a move Hudson knew was meant to stall. Eventually she said, "Okay, so obviously you're not some actor for hire of something. Temp is slick but she's not *that* slick or out of her mind. I just can't wrap my head around this... around *you*."

Monae probably peeped the look on Hudson's face, saw the confusion etched there and realized she hadn't clarified things at all. She took a deep breath and exhaled slowly.

"It makes no sense, does it?" she asked.

"If it's what you're feeling, yes it does. We just need to find the part of the equation where you can explain it to me so I understand."

"You see," she exclaimed. "That right there."

Hudson chuckled. "Call me Stevie Wonder, Nae, cause I ain't seeing it."

There were a few beats of silence before Monae spoke again. This time she didn't look directly at him. "I think it's time for me to tell you about my ex."

CHAPTER TWENTY-FIVE

Monae hated talking about Robert. She preferred to keep him tucked into the smallest corner of her mind and go about her life pretending he didn't exist or that they never met. God, she could have saved herself so much trouble if she'd sent the server back with the drink he'd ordered for her that first night they met. She liked to play off her experience with Robert like he was just a waste of her time but anyone close enough to her knew he left some scars. Ian ruined her trust in men and solidified her position that, as a general rule, men weren't shit but what Robert had done to her was more calculated, more insidious. He carefully and deliberately chipped away at her self-confidence and self-worth until she didn't recognize herself. Monae hadn't even understood what being gaslit meant until she'd put enough distance between her and the asshole to see what had been going on. She'd worked so damn hard and spent so much time putting those pieces back together but seeing clearly how jaded he made her perception about how people were treated in relationships was like the slap across the face that pushed her to finally end things between them.

"My ex didn't have much patience for my feelings," she told

Hudson with a small, wry smile. "He was charming when we first met but the little putdowns started soon after. Except, they didn't really seem *that* much like putdowns at the start. He seemed... helpful. Like when he suggested maybe I should use mouthwash so that making out first thing in the morning would be more palatable. He'd tell me that certain outfits would look better on someone with a different body type and certain colors made my skin look washed out. He'd say that sometimes the way I spoke or how loud I laughed was unbecoming of an attorney. He *hated* the way I danced in my chair when I enjoyed my food. He called it fucking childish."

Hudson's face was impassive for a while before he schooled his features into an expression Monae hadn't seen in all the time she'd known him... anger. Those warm, expressive brown eyes were hard, and his nostrils flared as he clenched his jaw.

She cleared her throat to hide the discomfort she was feeling but she forced herself to get everything out instead of retreating behind her unaffected mask like she wanted to. "I would get dressed up... outfit on point, hair laid, makeup slayed and feel so damn good about myself and then he'd walk in and point out wrinkles in my outfit, my lipstick not being the best shade and just send my mood plummeting right down. He was critical of everything from what I ate, my hobbies, how much I drank right down to the way I fucked... you name it. Eventually it started to feel like bullying so I would try to tell him how I felt but he would shut me down, tell me I was making no sense and ask me if I knew how hard I made it to love me."

Monae closed her eyes, her throat becoming tight as a barrage of the memories she thought were well hidden rushed over her. She opened her eyes when she felt Hudson's hand on her waist. He'd gotten down beside her chair so they were level with each other.

"You don't have to continue," he said. "I get it."

She shook her head. "No, let me finish. I feel so fucking stupid but it's best for me to get it out."

He looked around the shop and pointed to some booths in the corner where they could sit side by side.

"Let's go there," he suggested. "I hate watching you look so distressed feeling like I can't do anything to comfort you."

The small break for them to relocate themselves and for Hudson to go buy the bottle of water he insisted she needed was enough for Monae to get a better handle on her emotions.

"After a while I started thinking that maybe I *was* being difficult. Maybe he was just trying to look out for me and that feeling grew especially after he proposed. It was every girl's fairytale, but I couldn't help feeling trapped. I convinced myself I was just being an ungrateful bitch." Monae laughed bitterly. "Maybe *I* didn't convince myself. He played a huge role in me feeling that way. I think I was resigned to my fate until he embarrassed the shit out of me at a company event he'd escorted me to. My co-worker, Orlando, was praising my work on a case I was involved in and he made the comment that he was happy I managed to get it right because he knew how careless I often am with work things. I was livid because not only was the statement uncalled for, but it was also a fucking lie. When we went home I wouldn't back down about how stupid and disrespectful he was, no matter how much he tried to tell me I was overreacting. Every time he told me I was overreacting I just shouted louder. He warned me to stop shouting but I was beyond caring and when I didn't..."

Monae was pressed up against Hudson as he rubbed her back, but his movements stalled when her voice stopped.

"And when you didn't?" he asked, voice thick. "The next words to come out of your mouth will determine whether I'm just taking everything you told me to help me understand you and how you may react to things between us better or if I'm going to have to hunt this son-of-a-bitch down."

She shook her head. "He isn't worth it. But yeah, it's what

you think. When I wouldn't stop yelling, he slapped me. It's like he slapped the literal sense back into me because that was all it took. I left that apartment with nothing and didn't return to collect my things until two days later with a few of my cousins so he knew not to play with me. He accused me of being stubborn in not accepting his apology, comparing me breaking up with him to cutting off my nose *and* gouging out my eyeballs to spite my face but I didn't care. I was done with him. It took a lot of time and a lot of space for me to realize the number he did on me... the number he still continues to do on me, it seems."

Hudson kissed the side of her head and it was that small, tender act that did her in. She didn't even know where the tears were coming from or why she was crying but he sat there comforting her with little rubs and kisses as she got it all out.

"Tempest accused me of entering dating situations that I knew wouldn't go anywhere because I was afraid of getting close to someone again, but I told her she was tripping. I guess she's always damned right because why else would I be freaking the fuck out because I found someone I love being around, who makes me feel good and who treats me with the respect I honestly just made up my mind I'd never receive."

"I get you," Hudson said after a while. "And I'm down for moving as slow as you want to as long as we're moving in the same direction."

She laughed, swiping the tears from her eyes. "I'd like that."

"Good."

Monae welcomed the soft, sweet pressure of Hudson's lips as she felt most of the apprehension she'd been feeling melt away.

"On a real though," she said once they started gathering their things to leave. "You're hot, great in bed, successful and a sweetheart. Why are you single? Tell me now if you hide dead bodies under your bed."

Hudson laughed. "My relationships all ran their courses.

Evelyn, my last serious girlfriend, even invited me to her wedding with the man I'm pretty sure she cheated on me with."

Monae's mouth dropped open. "Please tell me you didn't go."

"Do I look like Bobo the Clown?" he asked.

Monae laughed hard, patting his cheek as she said. "Nah, baby. You're so much cuter."

And just like that they were laughing and joking as they continued exploring Grace Bay with Monae's heart feeling light and airy within her chest. *So damn easy*.

CHAPTER TWENTY-SIX

Hudson prided himself on being a very even keeled person. He tried his best to not allow shit to get to him because at the end of the day being upset very rarely helped solve the problem. His family members constantly teased him about his almost unflappable nature and one cousin, Michael, used to make a point out of doing little things just to irritate him with the hope he would eventually snap. Michael learned two things on the day he took things one step too far by being fresh with a woman Hudson had just started dating. Firstly, it was stupid to confuse his easy, laidback nature for being unable to stand up himself or those he cared about and, also, broken noses were a bitch to heal. It was likely that same easy, laidback nature that made Evelyn feel comfortable inviting him to her wedding and being genuinely surprised when he hadn't showed up. Russ used to clown him for never having a relationship end on bad note and would suck his teeth when Hudson explained it was because they had run their natural course. His cousin would roll his eyes and warn him that he'd stop acting like a fucking android when he finally met the woman who got under his skin. And Hudson had never understood what the hell Russ was getting on about... until Monae.

He'd felt more distress in the forty minutes it took for them to sort out Monae's reservations about a relationship between them than he had at the end of all his serious relationships combined. Then there was the rage that burned through his blood when he thought about her ex degrading her, laying his hands on her and eventually making her doubt what was happening between them because she didn't think she deserved a love that was easy. The anger had its own pulse as they went about the rest of their afternoon even when the easygoing vibe returned and laughter found its way back to Monae's eyes. She'd told him the asshole wasn't worth it but that didn't stop Hudson from really wanting to run into the bastard somewhere. His irritation only truly faded when they returned to the hotel and Monae shimmied out of the floral sundress she'd been wearing as soon as she crossed the room's threshold. He'd barely shut the door before he was staring at Monae's apple shaped ass. It was firm but with enough jiggle that he wanted to take a bite. So he did just that, dropping to his knees and pulling her soft ass cheek between his teeth. Monae yelped before she started laughing but his hands came to her thighs to hold her in place as he continued covering her soft flesh with little bites. There was only so long he could take with his face pressed so close to her pussy that he could feel the warmth while her intoxicating scent made him painfully hard. He inhaled deeply and his mouth immediately watered in anticipation of tasting her, but he continued his playful attention to her ass until he couldn't anymore. Hudson held as much of her ass cheeks as he could in his palms and massaged them before spanking them lightly, enjoying the way they jiggled before he spread them and licked his way down to what his tongue was craving. She was as wet as he expected her to be when his tongue slipped in between her soft, juicy flesh. He groaned into her sweetness and chuckled when Monae almost pitched herself forward.

"Easy there," he murmured against her, holding her thighs more firmly to keep her upright as he delved his tongue into her pussy again. Eating Monae out was a spiritual experience, pure fucking transcendence. There were no words to describe the pleasure he got from feeling Monae's hot, softness under his tongue, tasting her essence and hearing her mewling cries that grew in pitch and urgency until she shook so hard that he allowed her to fall against him and they both fell to the floor. He held her there for a few minutes trailing a line down her spine and massaging her already throbbing pussy until she begged him to stop. Then, he gathered her up in his arms and took her to the bed, anxious to feel her throbbing on his dick. Hudson lay on his side, turning her to face him and propping one of her legs on his waist as he slid into her pussy.

"Jesus," he groaned, pushing himself to the hilt inside her. She clenched him so tightly, Hudson was lightheaded as he brought his forehead to hers. He wanted to jackhammer his way to the release his body was desperate for, but he fought the urge. He fucked her slowly, relishing each gasp that fell from her lips and the way her eyes kept fluttering closed because she was overwhelmed by pleasure.

"Look at me, Nae Nae," he demanded, softly rocking his hips a little bit once he was fully buried in her. She opened her eyes for him but soon they were fluttering closed again.

"No, Nae Nae," he whispered. "Let me see those beautiful eyes of yours."

He wrapped his hands up in her hair and brought his mouth to hers, kissing her until the emotion that filled up his chest was too much for him to bear. She gazed at him, eyes wide with desire, as she turned her body a little so she could wrap her leg more tightly around his waist. He'd been prepared to continue letting the wave build with his slow, deep thrusts until the tsunami washed over them but then Monae brought her hand to his cheek, tipped her head back and moaned, "Fuck me, please."

Hudson couldn't do anything other than indulge his woman, gripping her ass and pulling her into him as he thrust fast and deep until Monae's fingers dug hard into his shoulders and his body tensed before he started his freefall to release. He groaned loudly while she screamed his name, dragging his lips across her cheek as they came together. And when Monae snuggled into him as they reveled in their post orgasm bliss, Hudson realized he was feeling something he'd never felt with another woman before her: complete.

"I don't think I've ever felt like this before."

Hudson was whispering even though the door to the balcony was closed and when he glanced in Monae was still dead to the world. Russ jerked his head back and chuckled. "A heart for the tinman, huh?"

"This is why I never come to you with anything."

Russ wasn't censored by Hudson's comment. Instead, he laughed even harder. "The man discovers his feelings and is suddenly touchy and shit."

"Aye, if you don't shut up," Hudson said. "I called you for advice and you're just over there acting the fool with your bigheaded ass."

He adjusted his phone so Russ could get a proper view of him sitting on the balcony, nursing a whiskey on ice while he enjoyed the balmy, evening breeze as Monae got her energy back. Russ was sprawled off on his and Tempest's couch holding the smartphone way above his head, still yet unwilling to stop teasing Hudson.

"Come let me get some of these in," he said. "I've watched you be Mr. Unflappable for so damn long that I'm happy as hell to see you pressed."

"It'd be your own family."

"On a real though," Russ said. "I understand how it feels to be completely knocked off your feet by love. One day you're going about your life happy, content and fulfilled and then the other second you meet someone and you know you'll never know true contentment again if they aren't by your side."

Hudson nodded. Russ was preaching the gospel truth and he was sitting in the very front pew.

"There's only one thing you can do, man," his cousin continued. "Don't second guess those feelings. Embrace them and hold on to her as tight as she'll allow."

He sat there for a few seconds, allowing the wisdom of Russ' words to sink in and then he asked, "Was the comment you made earlier referencing her last relationship?

Russ swiped his palm over his forehead. "Yeah, that was some gnarly shit. You'll never have to think twice about how Tempest feels about you. She loves Monae and Wynn fiercely and trusting you enough to take a shot at Whip's heart says a whole fucking lot."

Russ' statement sobered Hudson. He hadn't thought of the magnitude of Tempest advocating so strongly for a connection between him and her closest friend. Especially knowing how badly Monae had been hurt before.

"I'll do good by Nae," he said. "I won't ever put the look in her eyes that that other nigga did."

"Didn't think for a second you would but I gotta warn you that I'll sit back and watch both Tempest and Granny kick your ass if you do."

"And that is my cue to end this blasted call," Hudson chuckled. He started moving to end the video call, but his finger stalled over the disconnect button when Russ called his name.

"Yes?" he asked waiting for whatever foolishness Russ was about to say. His cousin smiled at him. "It feels good doesn't it?"

Hudson didn't have to think about his response. "It's the best thing I've ever felt."

CHAPTER TWENTY-SEVEN

She missed him.

Monae chuckled at the idea of missing a man who was just a few floors above her getting ready for their date. It was ridiculous but it didn't stop it from being true. She missed Hudson even though he'd kissed her goodbye and smacked her ass less than two hours before when she left to return to her room to get ready. She'd been able to distract herself from the pang of wistfulness she felt by having a scalding shower before oiling and then moisturizing her skin with her favorite body butter. She couldn't believe this was their last night at the resort. Monae wasn't happy about leaving the bubble she and Hudson created but she supposed reality had to enter the chat at some point. Speaking of reality, she'd barely placed the body butter back on the bedside table before her cell phone started ringing.

"Hey Temp," she chirped, popping in one of her earbuds so she could continue getting dressed.

"Don't *hey Temp* me after going radio silent for days," her friend huffed. "All it takes is some good dick and suddenly you forget the person who made this happen in the first place."

Monae held a bright yellow blouse against her chest and

surveyed herself in the mirror before returning to her suitcase and pulling out a coral jumpsuit instead.

"I was silent for a few hours, I don't know where you're coming talking about days," Monae chuckled. "But tell me, how long are you going to brag for? I need to know if I'll have any eyes left back in my sockets for how hard I'm going to have to roll them each time you mention being responsible for my relationship."

"*My relationship*," Tempest howled. "It be like that, huh? A whole ass relationship that wouldn't have come about if it wasn't for me."

"Tempest..."

"Don't Tempest me," her friend scolded. "I deserve to rejoice in this."

Monae fixed her mouth to respond but she heard a sound that stopped her in her tracks. She was still trying to figure out if she'd heard right when she heard it again.

"Tempest," she said softly. "Are you okay? Are you *crying*?"

Tempest sniffled again before she responded. "Of course I'm crying, bitch. Pregnancy hormones aren't a walk in the park and I'm so damn relieved."

Her exclamation surprised Monae. "Relieved?"

"Yeah, Whip. I had more riding on this than my need to be right. It was hard as your best friend watching someone with so much love to give keep choosing men who would be disappointments anyway because she was afraid of getting hurt. I know you've done the self-work needed to mostly work through what Robert's long necked ass put you through but sometimes the biggest component of true healing is being loved in a manner that brings home just how bad and toxic the love you'd been settling for was."

The rush of emotion that swept over Monae was hard to contain so she said, "You've said a mouthful."

"Of pure facts," Tempest added. "Hudson is just the sweetest, most collected, kindest soul and even before I realized how much your interests melded, I knew he'd be good for you. So, excuse me for being elated I was right."

"Trust me when I say you can't be more elated than me that your intuition was spot on," Monae said. "It's jarring getting everything I wanted when my heart didn't even realize it wanted it."

"Please don't," Tempest sniffed again. "My hormones cannot withstand hearing things like that.

Monae laughed. "I'm trying my best not to let fear dictate how I am receiving this but, Temp, it's hard. I'm waiting for the other shoe to drop. Could it really be *this* easy? It feels like a scam."

"A scam?" Tempest said. "Chile, the only scam that happened was getting you lovely folks together in the first place. Everything else is providence, fate, destiny... whatever you want to call it. And yes... it can really be *this* easy. The true scam is us being taught you must suffer for, in or through love. If anything gets hard it should be the world around you, but never your love. Love is the only thing in this world that's meant to be fucking easy. Just enjoy the shit out of what's happening between you and Hudson and stop waiting for the other shoe to drop. It won't. You're right where you're supposed to be."

Monae was speechless. "Wow, Tempest. You should get pregnant more often if it's going to make you so wise."

"You do a nice thing for bitch and she has the heart to still be sassy with you," Tempest complained. "I'm not staying here for the disrespect. I'm going to find Russ so he can come knock on the door of our baby's house a few times."

It took a few seconds before Monae made sense of what Tempest was saying. She screwed up her face. "You are so nasty."

"You've been so busy sitting on dick that you haven't responded to a single text in the group chat *you* reinstituted so miss me with the judgment." Tempest huffed. "I love you. Go 'head and continue enjoying your *relationship*."

Tempest chuckled a bit more before she disconnected the call. Monae shook her head and continued putting the finishing touches to the outfit she'd chosen before she scrolled through the group chat to find that Wynn and Tempest had, indeed, been roasting the shit out of her silence over the last few hours. She was in the process of firing off some responses when a firm knock at her door alerted her of Hudson's presence. And just like that her heart rate sped up and certain parts of her body were decidedly moister.

"Lord, help me," she muttered to herself as she grabbed her clutch and walked to the door on four-inch, black stilettos, determined to do exactly what Tempest advised.

CHAPTER TWENTY-EIGHT

There would come a time when Hudson wouldn't be bowled over by Monae's alluring beauty, but that time was not that night. He found it hard to gather his thoughts when the door swung open and she stepped out wearing a form fitting jumpsuit and high heels that had his mind wandering to her resting those heels on his shoulders as he lost himself in her pussy.

"Hey, babe," she said, her burgundy painted lips curving into a smile as she embraced him.

"You're so gorgeous," he said, licking his lips as he led her into the elevator. "Then again you'd make a wet paper bag look couture."

The musical lilt of her laughter filled the elevator. Monae tilted her chin up to him with an even wider smile stretching across her face. Her voice went all husky when she said, "The pussy's already yours, Hudson."

He brought his hands to either side of her waist and pulled her into him, crashing his lips against hers, kissing her until her lipstick smudged. "I don't just want your pussy, Nae. I need all of you."

Hudson wiped away some of the lipstick smeared just below

her bottom lip with his thumb. "I want your laughter and those smiles. I want you to trust me with your hopes, dreams and fears. I want you to trust me with your heart."

She leaned her head to the side. The smile was still plastered on her face but it matched the softness that crept into her eyes. She pulled her bottom lip through her teeth and Hudson sent out a prayer of gratitude into the Universe that she'd chosen to wear a jumpsuit. He would have been tempted to do something reckless if she'd been wearing an outfit that provided easy access.

"You know exactly what to say to make me go weak," she whispered, and he noticed how glassy her eyes were. He kissed her lips softly. "I tell you the truth."

"I must be insane because I feel like I'm already halfway to falling in love with you," Monae said with enough emotion in her voice to melt Hudson's entire soul. "And me trusting you enough to tell you that is such a confusing feeling."

He pulled her closer, kissing the top of her head when she rested her face against his shoulder. "You're not falling alone, Nae and I think I'm closer to the ground."

"It's a good thing I plan on catching you, then," she whispered against his chest and Hudson decided it was a good thing, indeed, because in those moments he realized he wasn't just falling in love with Monae. He was already there and he didn't want to be anywhere else.

~

They'd chosen to spend their last night dining in one of the fancier restaurants on the resort. A smiling server seated them on the patio that extended very close to the shoreline. It was a beautiful set up. The full moon was high in the sky, providing ambience that would not have been available with just the dim lighting of the restaurant. The sound of ocean waves crashing provided a steady cadence against the backdrop of the smooth jazz the restaurant played. The air smelled of all the secrets of the ocean and every so often Hudson's stomach growled when some delectable smell wafted out of the kitchen. And despite all the beauty, it still paled easily in comparison to the woman seated opposite him perusing the menu with a sexy amount of concentration. If Hudson had learned one thing about Monae during the trip, it was that she didn't play when it came to her food and he couldn't wait to explore some of his favorite restaurants back in New York with her. He told her this and a smile blossomed on her face.

"I can't wait to show you my favorite haunts too," she laughed. "But be warned, half of them are probably seafood restaurants."

He giggled. "Yeah, yeah. I know you're partial to your sea cockroaches."

Monae rolled her eyes and started debating the virtues of shrimp that he still couldn't see but he kept egging her on because he loved to see how worked up she got. Eventually, she realized everything she was saying was falling on deaf ears and retreated to her menu.

"You were wrong, you know," he said quietly after a few minutes passed.

She arched an eyebrow. "Wrong? About what?"

"Shrimp definitely isn't the best thing I've ever had in my mouth."

The red undertones of her caramel skin became even more pronounced as she tried to look anywhere but into his lust filled eyes.

"You and your flattery," she said. Hudson shook his head a little, understanding now that despite the confidence she exuded, Monae didn't know how to take a compliment and she hid her discomfort behind jokes.

"It's not flattery if it's true, Nae," he said. "I could spread you out on the table right now and I swear nothing they bring out of that kitchen would compare."

"Hudson!"

Her eyes had gone wide and that was when he realized the server had returned and was standing just off the side of him. He shrugged unapologetically. The truth was the truth.

"May I suggest the braised lamb," the young woman said with a little squeak, removing any doubt as to whether she'd overheard his comment.

"Sure," he said with his gaze still fixed on Monae. "Let's see how it compares."

CHAPTER TWENTY-NINE

Hudson was wicked as hell. How did he expect her to get through dinner without trying to climb him when he kept making comments like *that*, while looking like *that,* smelling like *that* and with memories of just how thoroughly he fucked her earlier still playing on her mind? He had her off balance and he seemed intent on keeping her that way. The sexual innuendo only slowed down once the food arrived and they started talking about the final things he had to put in place before he could open his gallery. The way she was excited and proud of him made it seem like she'd known him forever. But she supposed that made sense. She felt like she'd known him forever. He felt so damn familiar from the way his eyes squinted slightly before he grinned to how he tripped over his words when he was really excited about something and the exact depth of the dimples on either side of his cheek. Monae waited for the overwhelmed feeling to come but it didn't. She felt centered as she listened to Hudson speak about the benefits of different types of lighting and frames and the first collection he wanted to display.

"I can't wait to show you around so you can tell me what you think," he said excitedly.

"I don't know anything about art," she said.

He scoffed. "That's a lie. You have an eye for it. I watched you as we walked around that art and photo gallery in Grace Bay earlier. Besides, one of those photos you bought from me used to be my favorite."

"Used to be?"

"Mhm mhm," he said, moving to take a bite of his lamb. "I took one of you this morning that easily takes the number one spot."

Heat rushed to her cheeks as she asked. "Which one?"

She remembered earlier that morning after he'd fucked coherence out of her and she sprawled across the bed waiting for some semblance, *any semblance*, of normalcy to return to her body while he sat at the edge of the bed and caressed her sex.

"You have the most beautiful pussy," he'd whispered with the sort of reverence that made her turn her head to look up at him. He continued talking before she could say anything. "Can I photograph her?"

"Her?" she'd asked amused. "As in my yoni?"

He crawled between her legs, planting little kisses along the insides of her thighs before covering her with his mouth and bringing her already over stimulated body to yet another climax. He'd asked her again while she was still moaning and shaking from the orgasm that tore through her body. Maybe that was why she'd told him yes, or maybe it was because she'd expected him to whip out his smart phone and take a few photos to add to his spank bank. Monae, with her orgasm addled brain, forgot that Hudson was a photographer... a renowned one at that. He'd disappeared to his room and returned with *equipment*. She didn't have time to feel self-conscious as he got to work, gently maneuvering her legs while he took close shots of her pussy. Not with the compliments he kept raining down on her or the little kisses he would place on both sets of her lips when he was particularly pleased with whatever he was seeing on his camera's screen. He was careful to explain to her what he was doing from why a particular angle was preferred to when he was changing the aperture. Monae had leaned right into the sensuality of the entire process and when he finally showed her a few of the photos he liked the most she had to admit the sight of her moistened folds up close in black and white with the effects of the lighting and shadows made her hot as hell. And that was how Monae ended up ass up, face almost off the side of the bed as Hudson fucked out the pent-up desire their little impromptu session roused in him.

His soft chuckle snapped her back to reality and Monae realized she was holding the stem of her wine glass tight enough to break it.

"Get your mind out of the gutter, Nae Nae," he said, his voice overflowing with humor. He handed her his phone and showed her a photo of her on the balcony with her white robe on and knees pulled up to her chest as she sipped on coffee while watching the sunrise. The first blush of rays of sunlight were reflecting against her face and he'd captured all the serenity she'd felt in that moment.

"I have some edits to do to highlight texture and stuff, but for a raw photo this is stunning," he said. "I remember when we were eating at the airport, I couldn't help but think you'd make a perfect subject. My intuition was right. I can't wait to properly go through all of the photos I've taken of you."

"I was thinking you were talking about some of the photos you took on the boat," she said, trying to save face even though the memories of Hudson kneeling in front of her spread legs with his camera were making her throb.

"Sure you were," he said laughing. "That's why your breathing got all shallow and your eyes got so dazed I wanted to say fuck dessert and take you back to the room to recreate exactly what you were imagining."

Monae licked her lips and swallowed. "I mean... I see nothing wrong with that idea. In fact, it seems like a great one to me."

"Except I promised you we were going dancing tonight and I'm a man of my word," Hudson winked. "But afterwards that pretty ass of yours is fair game."

CHAPTER THIRTY

Fuck the dancing.

The thought crossed Hudson's mind no less than twenty times as they finished up their meal before walking hand in hand to the open-air dancefloor adjacent to the restaurant. He was happy he resisted the primal urge to get as close to Monae as was humanly possible when the live band started up just as they made their way into the middle of the dance floor and he pulled her into his arms. Sex with Monae was astounding but the intimacy he felt when it came to her went far deeper than flesh. Her light floral fragrance tickled his nose when he buried his face in her neck as they began swaying to the music. She felt so good in his arms. The live band was doing a damn good job of covering Giveon's 'Like I Want You' and Hudson immersed himself in the soulful ballad, the crisp ocean air, Monae's softness against his body and the tenderness his heart could barely contain. It was crazy to think he was just going about his life a week ago without the slightest inkling as to just how drastically it was about to change. He wasn't stupid enough to think things would always be smooth sailing between them both, but he was excited for all of it. Even the messy bits. There would be falling outs, but Hudson looked forward to the making up. He looked forward to convincing Monae by his actions that love was not unkind, it was not snarky, and it didn't break you down. It built you up in the best ways possible.

"I'm so happy Russ and Tempest acted the fool," Hudson whispered to Monae as the live band began its reggae set. "You awaken something in me that should be terrifying. It goes beyond all rationality that I should feel like this – *that I could feel like this* – but it feels like the most natural thing in the world."

She raised her chin and his heart beat hard when he saw the pure emotion in those hazel eyes.

"You're the best thing I've never asked for," she said. "I can't believe I kept turning down all of those blind dates. Imagine where we'd be right now if we'd met months ago."

He shook his head, placing a soft kiss to her forehead. "Nah. Everything in its own time. We got to where we are supposed to be."

He could taste the sweetness of the truth in his words but just in case he needed anymore confirmation, the band segued into their next tune. He couldn't help but laugh as the lead singer started crooning the lyrics of Bob Marley's 'Is This Love?'.

"Even the band be knowing," he laughed, swaying Monae to the beat. She laughed along with him as the band continued singing about a man telling a woman he wanted to love and treat her right. He pulled her even closer and pressed his cheek to hers when the band got to the refrain substituting the *is this love* for what he knew to true.

"This is love, this is love, this is love, this is love that I'm feeling," he sang softly. He wasn't really expecting a response from Monae, but his heart just about burst right out his chest when she stared up at him with solemn eyes and whispered, "Me too."

CHAPTER THIRTY-ONE

"You need any help in there?" Hudson called from where Monae had left him sitting on the balcony after they'd returned from dancing the night away. Monae tucked away the beautiful memories of swaying in the moonlight with the man who'd come to mean so much to her for whenever she needed happiness. She was sad their time on the island was coming to an end but as far as nights went, their last night was spectacular. Monae intended for them to end the night with fireworks.

"I'm good," she shouted back, returning her attention to the minibar where she'd just poured some hot water into a mug with a tea bag. She'd chosen peppermint because she thought the aroma was nice even though it didn't matter what was in the mug as long as it was hot. She rejoined Hudson on the balcony and placed the mug of tea next to the two tumblers she'd brought out. Hudson tried to pull her down to sit on him when she started making her way back into the hotel room, but she eased out of his embrace.

"I'll be right back," she grinned. "What do you want to drink? Tequila? Whiskey? I'll be having champagne."

His glance between her legs wasn't even subtle. Monae threw her head back and laughed. "You ain't slick."

He reached for her again and teased. "If you stop playing, parts of me could be."

Monae was still laughing when she returned briefly into the room to tie up her hair and get out of her clothes before she grabbed a bottle of champagne since Hudson clearly didn't have a preference and headed back to the balcony. He was still teasing her when she stepped back out on the balcony and he realized she was nude. He dragged his gaze up and down her body as she came to stand in front of him, making quick work of popping the bottle of champagne and pouring him a glass. She filled her own glass up with ice, pouring a small amount of champagne over it. She giggled at the curious look on Hudson's face when he compared the amount of champagne in his glass to the glass she held loosely in her hands.

"Ever heard what they say about a woman who pulls up her hair just before she gets on her knees?" she asked, smirking when Hudson took such a large gulp of champagne he almost choked on the bubbles.

"I can't say I have," he said when he could finally speak.

"Don't worry," Monae said kneeling in front of him. "Lemme show you."

She took her time unbuckling Hudson's pants and helping him out of them, leaning back to sit on her heels as he pulled his shirt over his head. That damn tattoo made her mouth water, but it wasn't just his sexy body that had her primed to give him the best head of his life. The unquenchable lust she felt for him became something primal when paired with the tender emotions that had settled in her chest. She wrapped her hand around his dick and stroked his hard length for a while as she brought her glass to her lips. She sipped on the champagne but spent most of the time swishing a cube of ice around her mouth until it completely melted. Then, she leaned forward and took Hudson's dick to the hilt. He jerked against her, his hands going to her shoulder as a surprised curse flew out of his mouth. She brought her lips back up to his tip making sure her tongue was pressed hard against his throbbing flesh on the way up. She applied gentle pressure to his balls as she took all of him in her mouth again before coming right back up, sucking his tip until his groans became louder. Monae stroked him with a tight fist as she reached for the mug of tea and took a huge gulp of the hot liquid, swirling it around before she swallowed making sure to leave a little bit of the warm tea in her mouth.

"What are you doing?" he asked and then moaned, "Oh, fuck" when Monae took his dick back into her mouth again. He was holding on to the arms of the chair he sat on as if they could save him from Monae's mouth and her constant shift between an icy tongue and wet heat. It wasn't long before he was thrusting upwards into Monae's mouth. She took a deep breath, relaxed her throat muscles and allowed him to fuck her mouth. Monae wanted to take Hudson's dick so far down her throat that he'd be able to feel the emotions she held for him in her heart. The way Hudson bucked against her, asked her if she intended to kill him, tried to undo her ponytail so he could fist her hair and eventually the way he moaned was enough for Monae to know she was succeeding. She pleasured him with her mouth until tears of determination ran down her face and her chest was wet with the saliva and pre-cum running down from her chin. She swallowed every bit of him when Hudson let out a guttural groan and spurted into her mouth, licking him clean and then sucking him dry. He was still panting when she finally rose from her knees, collapsed into the chair next to him and reached for her champagne.

"I," he started before stopping and trying to collect himself. "What the hell was what?"

He leaned his head against the back of the chair and chuckled. "I've never, ever felt anything like that. The ice? The tea? Where the hell did you learn how to do that?"

"Let's just say I was reading way more Eric Jerome Dickey when I was thirteen than I should've been at that age."

"Word? You learned that trick in a romance novel?"

She nodded, thinking about how scandalized she'd been when she first read that scene. "Yeah. The ice, at least. I didn't realize I'd stumbled upon something useful until I was much older. The warm tea, though? That was me putting my own spin on it."

"Damn. I'm gonna need to get me a few copies to see what the maestro can pass down about eating pussy."

She batted her eyelashes at him and flashed him an exaggeratedly coy smile. "From where me and my pussy are sitting, you're the one who should have a master class."

"You and your pussy sitting too far away," Hudson said patting his lap where his dick was already starting to get hard again.

Monae grinned wickedly at him. "We don't need to be told twice."

CHAPTER THIRTY-TWO

Hudson's brain was fried. He glanced down at his dick happily bobbing in front of him surprised that it recovered so quickly. Monae had completely demolished him with that tongue of hers. His balls tingled just thinking about it. She rose from her chair and crossed the small space between them, thankfully pulling her hair down from her ponytail so that it fell to her shoulders. She straddled him and he sighed with relief when he slid into her tight, wet warmth. He fisted her hair, brought her mouth to his and kissed her hungrily as she slowly found her rhythm, rising all the way up off his dick before slamming herself back down on him then rotating her hips in small tight circles that had him taking deep breaths so they didn't have a second round of her overwhelming him so damn much that he nutted too quickly. Their tongues lashed aggressively as she rode him faster and harder while he traced his fingers along her back before grabbing her ass so he could hold himself in place deep inside her until the first stirrings of his orgasm began fading away. It was late as hell and even though they had an early ass flight in the morning he wasn't ready to let her go.

"Stand up for me," he murmured into her neck, grasping her

thighs to steady her on her feet as he also rose. He wasn't surprised to find himself a little bit unsteady on his feet as he turned Monae to face the balcony and raised one of her legs to rest on the ledge. He thrust into her in a smooth, hard motion, bringing one hand between her legs and massaging her clit as he held her thigh to steady her. Hudson kissed the back of her neck as his thrusts picked up pace. Damn. How did he get so lucky? This was the closest to perfect as life could be, feeling the woman of his dreams' pussy clench and throb around his dick as he made love to her under the stars. She felt so good that his toes curled with every stroke.

"Cum for me, Nae," he whispered fiercely against her ear when her cries became so loud and desperate that he knew she was close. It took only a few more deep thrusts before he could feel her gushing all over his dick and Hudson couldn't hold out any longer. His body shook under the force of his release and it took all his strength to hoist Monae up in his arms and bring her back to the bed. She was already halfway dozing when he returned from the bathroom with a warm rag to clean her up. She snuggled right into him when he finally made his way to bed and soon her deep, steady breaths let him know she'd fallen asleep. His body was depleted but his heart was so damn full when he considered that this blind date was quite likely the blind date to end the possibility of all others. Hudson kissed the top of her head and pulled Monae even closer. He'd found his forever Valentine and he was never letting her go.

CHAPTER THIRTY-THREE

Monae couldn't get over how damned adorable Hudson was when he slept. She dropped a small kiss on his pouty lips and didn't hesitate to deepen the kiss when he pulled her closer.

"Good morning, gorgeous," he whispered as his lips curved into a sexy smile that made Monae want to straddle his face. She glanced at the bedside clock wondering if she had enough time to make that happen before swearing under her breath.

"We're late," she said jumping from the bed as Hudson checked his phone and swore as well. Monae laughed at the irony of her ending the trip just as it began, frantically trying her best to get to the airport on time. Her heart stuttered in her chest when it hit her how differently this trip was ending as well. Hudson was trying to help her pack up her stuff before he even thought of returning to his room where he was, thankfully, already packed. She'd done three quick walkthroughs of the room and then had a quick shower and hastily pulled on a sweater and a comfortable pair of pants. She didn't even bother trying to tame the mess her hair was before she hurried downstairs to meet Hudson. He thrust a cup of coffee into her hands as soon as she was close to him and she leaned up to give him a grateful kiss. If she wasn't already sure she loved him, she would've known then as she sipped on the hot, nutty liquid while Hudson helped the taxi driver load the bags into the vehicle. She didn't allow herself to calm down until they were checked in and could rest secure in the knowledge they wouldn't miss their flight. Monae was surprised by how panicked she was at the thought of missing the flight when she would have gladly stayed in Providenciales and the little bubble she and Hudson had created. Reality was fast approaching and as optimistic as she felt about what their relationship could grow into, she couldn't fight the unease she felt at the pressures real life would bring.

"You good?" Hudson asked. He'd been flicking through a magazine while they waited for the plane to start boarding. She wasn't surprised he'd picked up on the change in her energy even though she was trying her hardest not to let on that anything was wrong.

"I hate it that we have to leave here," she admitted. "We're back to the banality of everyday life."

He laced his fingers through hers and Monae rested her head on his shoulder, throwing both feet over his as he pulled her in for a hug.

"I look forward to the banality of everyday life," he said. "The midweek dates, grocery runs, trying to get our calendars to sync up, waking up next to you, listening to you vent about work, rediscovering the city through your eyes, weekend getaways, the stupid little fights and the hot make up sessions. I can't wait for that."

She smiled into Hudson's chest, imagining him cuddled up with her watching an entire season of some TV show while eating takeout.

"You're not wrong," she said. "I guess I'm just a bit bummed that this is ending."

"You shouldn't be," he said in a voice filled with confidence.

He tipped her chin up and pressed a soft, sweet kiss against her lips. "The best is yet to come."

#THE END

AFTERWORD

I had a lot of fun with Monae and Hudson. Hudson was a real star. I also really enjoyed revisiting Tempest and Russ, even if it was only briefly.

If you liked this book, please think about rating it and/or leaving a review on Amazon and/or Goodreads and telling your friends about it. Word of mouth is so important for indie authors.

Peace. Love. Light.
Rilzy

ABOUT THE AUTHOR

Rilzy Adams believes all you need is love. Or, at least it should. She may, or may not, be a huge Beatles fan. She spends too much time living in her head watching the romantic lives of her 'imaginary friends' play out and then being the chatty friend to tell the world about them. When she isn't living in her head, she must show up to work every day and be a lawyer. She resides, with her two dogs, on an island in the middle of the Caribbean Sea, which is perfect for her sun addiction, love affair with Prosecco and sushi worship.

For information on new releases, promotions and more:
Join the Mailing List
Visit her website at: www.rilzywrites.com

ALSO BY RILZY ADAMS

FALLING LIKE A JOHNSON SERIES

The Gift (Jaxon and Maya)

Will You Be Mine? (JT and Hallie)

Just One More Time (Orlando and Katrina)

When Love Ignites (Jasmine and Alec)

The Sweetest Escape (Jasper and Reign)

Yours Always (Orlando and Katrina)

UNEXPECTED LOVERS SERIES

Go Deep (Xander and Navaya)

Deeper (Xander and Navaya's wedding story)

LOVE ON THE ROCK BOOKS

Twelve Dates of Christmas (Zia and Rashad)

You, Me + Baby (Fran and Andre)

Brand New (Regina and Quentin)

Birthday Shot (Shae and Kofi)

SINGLES

Off Key (Zoe and Liam)

Love in the Time of Corona (Alyssa and Kingsley)

ATE (Tempest and Russ)

Ho! Ho! Ho! (Myla and JB)

SHORT STORY COMPILATIONS

Love Bites – A Collection of Short Stories

Printed in Great Britain
by Amazon

82574196R00082